Making People Happy

Thompson Buchanan

Alpha Editions

This edition published in 2022

ISBN : 9789356716032

Design and Setting By
Alpha Editions
www.alphaedis.com
Email - info@alphaedis.com

Contents

CHAPTER I

The bride hammered the table desperately with her gavel. In vain! The room was in pandemonium.

The lithe and curving form of the girl—for she was only twenty, although already a wife—was tense now as she stood there in her own drawing-room, stoutly battling to bring order out of chaos. Usually the creamy pallor of her cheeks was only most daintily touched with rose: at this moment the crimson of excitement burned fiercely. Usually her eyes of amber were soft and tender: now they were glowing with an indignation that was half-wrath.

Still the bride beat a tattoo of outraged authority with the gavel, wholly without avail. The confusion that reigned in the charming drawing-room of Cicily Hamilton did but grow momently the more confounded. The Civitas Club was in full operation, and would brook no restraint. Each of the twelve women, who were ranged in chairs facing the presiding officer, was talking loudly and swiftly and incessantly. None paid the slightest heed to the frantic appeal of the gavel.... Then, at last, the harassed bride reached the limit of endurance. She threw the gavel from her angrily, and cried out shrilly above the massed clamor of the other voices:

"If you don't stop," she declared vehemently, "I'll never speak to one of you again!"

That wail of protest was not without its effect. There came a chorus of ejaculations; but the monologues had been efficiently interrupted, and the attention of the garrulous twelve was finally given to the presiding officer. For a moment, silence fell. It was broken by Ruth Howard, a girl with large, soulful brown eyes and a manner of rapt earnestness, who uttered her plaint in a tone of exceeding bitterness:

"And we came together in love!"

At that, Cicily Hamilton forgot her petulance over the tumult, and smiled with the sweetness that was characteristic of her.

"Really, you know," she confessed, almost contritely, "I don't like to lecture you in my own house; but we came together for a serious purpose, and you are just as rude as if you'd merely come to tea."

One of the women in the front row of chairs uttered a crisp cry of approval. This was Mrs. Flynn, a visiting militant suffragette from England. Her aggressive manner and the eager expression of her narrow face with the gleaming black eyes declared that this woman of forty was by nature a fighter who delighted in the fray.

"Yes; Mrs. Hamilton is right," was her caustic comment. "We are forgetting our great work—the emancipation of woman!"

Cicily beamed approval on the speaker; but she inverted the other's phrase:

"Yes," she agreed, "our great work—the subjugation of man!"

The statement was not, however, allowed to go unchallenged. Helen Johnson, who was well along in the twenties at least, and still a spinster, prided herself on her powers of conquest, despite the fact that she had no husband to show for it. So, now, she spoke with an air of languid superiority:

"Oh, we've already accomplished the subjugation of man," she drawled, and smiled complacently.

"Some of us have," Cicily retorted; and the accent on the first word pointed the allusion.

"Oh, hush, dear!" The chiding whisper came from Mrs. Delancy, a gray-haired woman of sixty-five, somewhat inclined to stoutness and having a handsome, kindly face. She was the aunt of Cicily, and had reared the motherless girl in her New York home. Now, on a visit to her niece, the bride of a year, she found herself inevitably involved in the somewhat turbulent session of the Civitas Club, with which as yet she enjoyed no great amount of sympathy. Her position in the chair nearest the presiding officer gave her opportunity to voice the rebuke without being overheard by anyone save the militant Mrs. Flynn, who smiled covertly.

Cicily bent forward, and spoke softly to her aunt's ear:

"I just had to say it, auntie," she avowed happily. "You know, she tried her hardest to catch Charles."

Mrs. Morton, a middle-aged society woman, who displayed sporadic interest in the cause of woman during the dull season, now rose from the chair immediately behind Mrs. Flynn, and spoke with a tone of great decisiveness:

"Yes, ladies of the Civitas Club, Mrs. Flynn is perfectly right." She indicated the identity of the militant suffragette, who was a stranger to most of those in the company, by a sweeping gesture. "It is our duty to follow firmly on the path which our sister has indicated toward the emancipation of woman. We should get the club started at once, and the work done immediately. Lent will be over soon, and then there will be no time for it."

"Yes, indeed," Cicily agreed enthusiastically, as Mrs. Morton again subsided into her chair; "let's get the club going right away." The presiding officer hesitated for a moment, fumbling among the papers on the table. "What's the name—? Oh, here it is!" she concluded, lifting a sheet from the litter before her. "Listen! It's the Civitas Society for the Uplift of Woman and for Encouraging the Spread of Social Equality among the Masses."

As this gratifyingly sonorous designation was enunciated by Cicily in her most impressive voice, the members of the club straightened in their places with obvious pride, and there was a burst of hand-clapping. Ruth Howard's great eyes rolled delightedly.

"Oh," she gushed, "isn't it a darling duck of a name! Let's see—the Vivitas Society for—for—what is it for, anyhow?"

Cicily came to the rescue of the forgetful zealot.

"It's for the purpose of bringing men and women closer together," she explained with dignity.

Miss Johnson gushed approval with her usual air of coquettish superiority.

"Oh, read it again, Cicily," she urged. "It's so inspiring!"

"Yes, do read it again," a number of enthusiasts cried in chorus.

The presiding officer was on the point of complying with the demand for a repetition of the sonorous nomenclature:

"The Civitas Society for—" she began, with stately emphasis. But she broke off abruptly, under the impulse of a change in mood. "Oh, what's the use?" she questioned flippantly. "You'll all get copies of it in full in your mail to-morrow morning." Mightily pleased with this labor-saving expedient, Cicily beamed on her fellow club-members. "What next?" she inquired, amiably.

Mrs. Carrington rose to her feet, and addressed the assembly with that dignity befitting one deeply experienced in parliamentary exercises.

"Having voted on the name," she remarked ponderously, evidently undisturbed by the exceedingly informal nature of the voting, if such it could be called, "I think it is now time for us to start the society." She stared condescendingly through her lorgnette at the duly impressed company, and sank back into her chair.

There were many exclamations of assent to Mrs. Carrington's timely proposal, and much nodding of heads. Plainly, the ladies were minded to start the society forthwith. Unhappily, however, there remained an obstacle to the accomplishment of that desirable end—a somewhat general ignorance as to the proper method of procedure. Ruth Howard turned the gaze of her large brown eyes wistfully on Mrs. Carrington, and voiced the dilemma by a question:

"How do we start?" she asked, in a tone of gentle wonder.

Before Mrs. Carrington could formulate a reply to this pertinent interrogation, the militant suffragette from England began an oration.

"The start of a great movement such as is this," Mrs. Flynn declaimed, "is like unto the start of a great race, or the start of a noble sport; it is like—"

Cicily was so enthusiastic over this explanation that she interrupted the speaker in order to demonstrate the fact that she understood the matter perfectly.

"You mean," she exclaimed joyously, "that you blow a whistle, or shoot a pistol!"

This appalling ignorance of parliamentary tactics induced some of the more learned to ill-concealed titters; Miss Johnson permitted herself to laugh in a gurgling note that she affected. But it was Mrs. Carrington who took it on herself to utter a veiled rebuke.

"I fear Mrs. Hamilton has not been a member of many clubs," she remarked, icily.

At Miss Johnson's open flouting, Cicily had flushed painfully. Now, however, she was ready with a retort to Mrs. Carrington's implied criticism:

"Oh, on the contrary!" she exclaimed. "Why, I was chief rooter of the Pi Iota Gammas, when I went to boarding-school at Briarcliff."

Miss Johnson spoke with dangerous suavity of manner:

"Then, my dear, since you were one of the Pigs—pardon my using the English of it, but I never could pronounce those Greek letters—"

"Of course not," Cicily interrupted, with her sweetest smile. "I remember, Helen, dear: you had no chance to practise, not having belonged at Briarcliff."

Kindly Mrs. Delancy was on nettles during the passage of the gently spoken, but none the less acrimonious, remarks between her niece and Miss Johnson. She was well aware of Cicily's deep-seated aversion for the coquettish older woman, who had not scrupled to employ all her arts to win away another's lover. That she had failed utterly in her efforts to make an impression on the heart of Charles Hamilton did not mitigate the offense in the estimation of the bride. So strong was Cicily's feeling, indeed, and so impulsive her temperament, that the aunt was really alarmed for fear of an open rupture between the two young women, for Helen Johnson had a venomous tongue, and a liking for its employment. So, now, Mrs. Delancy hastened to break off a conversation that threatened disaster.

"Let us select the officers, the first thing," she suggested, rising for the sake of effectiveness in securing attention to herself. "It is, I believe, usual in clubs to have officers, and, for that reason, it seems to me that it would be well to select officers for this club, here and now." Mrs. Delancy reseated herself, well satisfied with her effort, for there was a general buzz of interest among her auditors.

Cicily, with the lively change of moods that was distinctive of her, was instantly smiling again, but now with sincerity. Without a moment of hesitation, she accepted the suggestion, and acted upon it. She turned toward Mrs. Carrington, and addressed her words to that dignified person:

"Yes, indeed," she declared gladly, "I accept the suggestion.... Won't you be president, Mrs. Carrington?"

The important lady was obviously delighted by this suggestion. She smiled radiantly, and she fairly preened herself so that the spangles on her black gown shone proudly.

"Thank you, my dear Mrs. Hamilton," she replied tenderly, with a pretense of humility that failed completely. "But I believe there are certain formalities that are ordinarily observed—I believe that it is a matter of selection by the club as a whole. Of course, if—" She paused expectantly, and regarded those about her with a smile that was weighted with suggestion.

Cicily was somewhat perturbed by the error into which she had fallen. It occurred to her that Helen Johnson might here find another opportunity for the gratification of malice. A glance showed that this detestable young woman was in fact exchanging pitying glances with Mrs. Flynn. Cicily was flushed with chagrin, as she spoke falteringly, with an apologetic inflection:

"Oh, the president has to be elected? I beg your pardon! I thought it was like the army, and—went by age."

At this unfortunate explanation, the simper of gratified vanity on Mrs. Carrington's features vanished as if by magic. She stiffened visibly, as she acridly ejaculated a single word:

"Really!" The inflection was scathing.

Mrs. Flynn, who was smiling complacently over the evident confusion of Cicily, now stood up to instruct that unhappy presiding officer:

"No, indeed, Mrs. Hamilton," she announced with great earnestness, "for the most part, it is the young women, even young wives no older than yourself oftentimes, who are at the front, fighting gloriously the battle of all women in this great movement.... At least, that is the way in England." She paused and bridled as she surveyed the attentive company, her manner full of self-content. "There, I may say, the youngest and the most beautiful women have been the leaders in the fray. Ahem!"

Cicily did not hesitate to remove all ambiguity from the utterance of the militant suffragette with the sallow, narrow face.

"And you were a great leader, were you not, Mrs. Flynn?" she demanded, bluntly.

There were covert smiles from the other women; but the Englishwoman was frankly gratified by the implication. She was smiling with pleasure as she answered:

"I may say truthfully that I know the inside of almost every police-station in London."

At this startling announcement, uttered with every appearance of pride, the suffragette's hearers displayed their amazement by exclamations and gestures. Mrs. Carrington especially made manifest the fact that she had scant patience with this manner of martyrdom in the cause of woman's emancipation.

"My dear Mrs. Flynn," she said, with a hint of contempt in her voice, "here in America, we do not think that getting into jail is necessarily a cause for pride." There were murmurs of assent from most of the others; but Mrs. Flynn herself was in no wise daunted.

"Well, then, it should be," she retorted, briskly. "Zeal is the watchword!"

"I think that Mrs. Flynn should be president," Miss Johnson cried with sudden enthusiasm. "She has suffered in the cause!"

"Oh, for that matter," interjected Mrs. Morton flippantly, "most of us are married." It was known to all those whom she addressed, save perhaps the Englishwoman, that at the age of forty Mrs. Morton had undergone two divorces, and that she was now living wretchedly with a third husband, so she spoke with the authority of one having had sufficient experience.

But Mrs. Flynn was too much interested in her own harrowing experiences to be diverted by cynical raillery.

"The last time I went to jail," she related, "I had chained myself to the gallery in the House of Commons, and, when they tried to release me, I bit a policeman—hard!"

"Oh, you man-eater!" It was Cicily who uttered the exclamation, half-reproachfully, half-banteringly.

"I fail to see why, if one should prefer even Chicago roast beef to an Irish policeman, that should be held against one." This was Mrs. Carrington's indignant comment on the narrative of the mordant martyr.

The remark affected Mrs. Flynn, however, in a fashion totally unexpected. She cried out in genuine horror and disgust over the suggested idea.

"Good heavens! Do you imagine I would ever bite an Irish policeman?"

"If not," Mrs. Carrington rejoined slyly, "you will have very small opportunity in New York for the exercise of your very peculiar talents."

Cicily interposed a remark concerning the appetizing charms of some of the mounted policemen. It seemed to her that the conversation between the two older women had reached a point where interruption were the course of prudence. "I think we had better do some more business, now," she added hastily, with an appealing glance toward her aunt.

Mrs. Delancy rose to the emergency on the instant.

"By all means," she urged. "Let us get on with the business. We haven't been going ahead very fast, it seems to me. Why not elect the officers right away?"

Once again, the entire company became agog with interest over the project of securing duly authorized officials. There were murmured conversations, confidential whisperings. As Ruth Howard earnestly declared, it was so exciting—a real election. A stealthy canvas of candidates was in full swing. The names of Mrs. Flynn and of Mrs. Carrington were heard oftenest. Incidentally, certain sentences threw light on individual methods of determining executive merit. A prim spinster shook her head violently over some suggestion from the woman beside her. "No, my dear," she replied aggressively, "I certainly shall not vote for her—vote for a woman who wears a transformation? No, indeed!"... Cicily improved the interval of general bustle to inquire secretly of her aunt as to the possible shininess of her nose. "It always gets shiny when I get excited," she explained, ruefully. As a matter of fact, there was nothing whatever the matter with that dainty feature, which had a fascination all its own by reason of the fact that one was forever wondering whether it was classically straight or up-tilted just the least infinitesimal fraction.

It was Mrs. Morton who first took energetic action toward an election. She stood up, and spoke with a tone of finality:

"I think that dear Mrs. Carrington would make a splendid officer. I nominate dear Mrs. Carrington for our president."

"Did you hear that, Mrs. Carrington?" Cicily inquired, with a pleased smile for the one thus honored. "You're nominated."

"Oh, it's so thrilling!" Ruth Howard exclaimed, with irrepressible enthusiasm.

But Miss Johnson, to whom Ruth particularly addressed herself, had on occasion been unmercifully snubbed by Mrs. Carrington. In consequence, now, she showed no sign of sympathy with her companion's emotion. On the contrary, she sniffed indignantly, and muttered something about "that woman!"

Meantime, Mrs. Morton was waxing restless over the fact that things remained at a standstill, despite the nomination she had made. She rose to her feet, and surveyed the company with a glance eloquent of haughty surprise.

"I am waiting for a second to my motion," she remarked, icily. Then, as there was no audible response to this information, she added with rising indignation: "Well, really!" There was a wealth of contemptuous reproach in the tone.

The effect on the susceptible Cicily was instantaneous. With her customary impulsiveness, and her eagerness to do the right thing for any and all persons, she felt that she herself had been woefully remiss in not having hurried to Mrs. Morton's support at once. So, to make amends, she spoke with vivacity:

"Oh, I second it!... Mrs. Carrington," she continued, turning to the gratified candidate, "you're seconded." She was rewarded for her conduct by a stately bow of thanks from Mrs. Morton. Half a dozen others, taking their cue from the presiding officer, noisily cried out in seconding the candidacy of Mrs. Carrington, whereat Mrs. Morton grew flushed with pleasure, and was moved to consummate the affair without a moment's delay.

"I move that the election of Mrs. Carrington as president be now made, and also that the election be made unanimous," she demanded, with much unction in her voice. She smiled persuasively at the presiding officer as she concluded: "Won't you put that motion, my dear?"

Cicily rose to the occasion with an access of becoming dignity.

"It is moved and seconded," she announced loudly, "that Mrs. Carrington be elected president of this club. All in favor of this motion—"

"One moment, please," Miss Johnson interrupted, excitedly. "Madam Chairman, I move that Mrs. Flynn, the great, the tried, the proven, the trusted crusader in the cause of women, from England, be elected president, and that her election be made unanimous." She paused to turn to Ruth, whom she addressed in a fierce whisper: "If you don't second me, I'll never speak to you again."

"Oh, I second you," Ruth cried, anxiously. "Of course, I second you."

But, by this time, Cicily had come to a realization of the fact that the other women present were every whit as ignorant of parliamentary law as was she herself. So, in this emergency, she did not scruple to make audacious retort. She answered with exceeding blandness:

"But, you see, Miss Johnson, there's already a motion before the house."

Thereupon, Mrs. Morton hastened valiantly to her own support.

"Yes, indeed," she declared, haughtily; "my motion was first. I must insist that it be voted upon. If Miss Johnson wished to have an imported English president for our American society, she should have nominated Mrs. Flynn first." She made direct appeal to the presiding officer. "Am I not right, dear?"

Cicily beamed on Mrs. Morton, and was about to reply, when a sudden thought came to her that did greater credit to her ingenuity than to her executive knowledge. Forthwith, she beamed, somewhat hypocritically, on Miss Johnson in turn.

"Yes, certainly," she affirmed; "I'm sure you're both quite right."

"Thank you, Madam Chairman, for agreeing with me," Miss Johnson replied, placated by Cicily's unexpected amiability toward her. "My motion also is before the house, and I insist that it be voted on. Mrs. Flynn has been seconded."

There was a spirit of hostility in the manner with which Miss Johnson and Mrs. Morton faced each other that boded ill for peace. The rival candidates sat in rigid erectness, disdainfully aloof while their supporters wrangled. The whisperings of the others suggested a growing acrimoniousness of debate. That earnest maiden, Ruth, was alarmed by the tension of strife.

"I think I'd rather go," she faltered. "I'm afraid you're going to quarrel, Helen."

But the resources of Cicily's inspiration were by no means ended. She waved a conciliatory hand toward the adversaries, and spoke with an air of finality that produced an instantaneous effect as of oil on troubled waters.

"I'll tell you: I'll put one motion, and the other can be an amendment." At this profound suggestion, the whole company breathed a sigh of relief. Only Ruth appeared somewhat puzzled.

"What's an amendment?" she questioned frankly, while the others regarded her with evident scorn for such ignorance.

"An amendment, Ruth," the presiding officer explained patiently, "is—is—oh, just listen, and don't interrupt the proceedings, and you'll know all about it in a few minutes." She beamed once again, first on Mrs. Morton and then on Miss Johnson. "Which of you would rather be the amendment?" she inquired.

Mrs. Morton, as became her years, was first to make reply.

"It's entirely immaterial to me, just so my motion is put."

Miss Johnson adopted a manner that was not without signs of heroic self-sacrifice.

"I'll be the amendment," were her words. With that, she bowed very formally to Mrs. Morton, who returned the salute with a fine dignity, after which the two at last subsided into their chairs.

Cicily was elated with the subtle manner in which she had evolved order out of chaos. Her eyes glowed with pride, and the flush in her cheeks deepened. There was an added music in her voice, as she once more addressed the company.

"Splendid!" she ejaculated. "Now, all in favor of Mrs. Motion's morton—I mean Mrs. Morton's motion, please say ay!"

In a clear, ringing voice she led the chorus in the affirmative. Yes, every woman present, including the presiding officer, voted an enthusiastic ay, whereupon Cicily declared the motion carried; and Mrs. Morton rose and said: "Thank you, ladies." Next, Mrs. Carrington stood up, placed a hand on her heart, and expressed her appreciation of the honor done her: "I deeply thank you, ladies." The incident was fittingly concluded by an outburst of applause in which all the club joined, although Ruth beat her palms in rather a bewildered manner.... Cicily immediately entered on the new phase of the situation.

"Now, all in favor of Miss Johnson's amendment, please say ay," she directed. Again, she led the chorus in the affirmative, and the entire company joined in the vote without a dissenting voice. "Amendment carried," the presiding officer announced, gleefully. It was now the turn of Miss Johnson to rise and offer her thanks, and Mrs. Flynn followed, saying, very neatly: "From over the sea, I thank you." The usual applause was of the heartiest.... But Cicily was still energetic.

"Now, all in favor of the motion and of the amendment, please say ay," she requested. For the third time, she led the chorus, and the vote was unopposedly affirmative. "The motion and the amendment are carried unanimously," Cicily announced, and the hand clapping sounded a happy content on the part of the Civitas Club.

Afterward, came a little intermission of conversation in which was expressed much appreciation of the efficiency of the club in carrying on its session. "It all goes to show how businesslike women can be," Mrs. Carrington remarked, triumphantly. Mrs. Flynn was even more emphatic. "I've never seen a meeting more gloriously typical of our great cause." The tribute was welcomed with a buzz of assent.... But, finally, there came a lull in the talking. It was broken by Mrs. Delancy, who spoke thoughtlessly out of a confused mind, with no suspicion as to the sinister effect to be wrought by her words:

"Who's elected?" was her simple question.

There was a moment of amazed silence, in which the members of the club stared at one another with widened eyes. It was broken very speedily, however, by Mrs. Carrington, who rose to her feet with more activity of movement than was customary to her dignified bearing.

"I have the honor," she stated, sharply.

Instantly, Mrs. Flynn, the militant suffragette, was up, her face belligerent.

"Pardon me, but the honor belongs to me," she snapped, regarding the first claimant with a fierce indignation that was returned in kind. Most of the others were too confounded for speech, but Mrs. Morton rose to support her candidate's claims.

"Pray pardon me," she began placatingly, "but probably Mrs. Flynn does not understand. The interpretation of parliamentary law in England may be quite different. Probably, it is. The customs of that country vary widely from ours in many respects. So, they probably do in the matter of elections in clubs. Now, I belong to ten clubs—American clubs—and I assure you that, according to the parliamentary law in every one of those ten clubs, Mrs. Carrington is certainly elected."

This advocacy was, naturally, a challenge to Miss Johnson, who promptly rose up to champion her own candidate.

"Mrs. Carrington, I am sure, has no desire to take advantage of a distinguished stranger within our gates—and one who has served as gloriously in the cause as Mrs. Flynn—but, even if someone—" she regarded Mrs. Morton with great significance—"I say, even if someone should wish to take unfair advantage of a technicality, it would be altogether impossible, for my amendment to the original motion was carried—unanimously! Mrs. Flynn is the president of the club, duly elected."

Some hazy notion of parliamentary procedure moved Mrs. Flynn to a suggestion.

"I think the matter might best be settled by the chair," she said, doubtfully. "The chair put the motion. Let us then leave the decision to Madam Chairman." Mrs. Carrington nodded a stately agreement to the proposal, and the company as a whole appeared vastly relieved, with the exceptions of Miss Johnson, who sniffed defiantly, and of Ruth, who appeared more than ever bewildered by the succession of events.

Now, at last, Cicily felt herself baffled by the crisis of her own making. She looked from one to another with reproach in her amber eyes.

"But—but you cannot expect me to decide between my guests," she espostulated. There was appeal for relief in the pathetic droop of the scarlet lips of the bride, but it was of no avail. The company asserted with vehemence that she must render the decision in this unfortunate dilemma.... And, again, the angel of inspiration whispered a solution of the difficulty. Impulsive as ever, a radiant smile curved her mouth, and her eyes shone happily.

"Very well," she yielded. "Since you insist on putting your hostess in such an unfortunate position, I decide that it is up to the ladies themselves. Which one wishes to take the office, to force herself forward against the wishes of the other?" She cast a seemingly guileless glance of inquiry first on Mrs. Carrington, then on Mrs. Flynn, who simultaneously uttered exclamations of indignation at the imputation thus laid upon them.

Mrs. Carrington was quick to make explicit answer.

"If the ladies of the club do not desire me to be president, I must decline to accept the office, in spite of a unanimous vote. If, however—" She broke off to stare accusingly at her rival, then about the room in search of encouragement for her claims.

Mrs. Flynn took advantage of the opportunity for speech in her own behalf.

"Naturally, as a stranger, I hesitate to force myself forward, even though my record is such that it is hard to see how any opposition could possibly develop against me. However—"

"Of course, Mrs. Carrington is elected," Mrs. Morton interrupted.

At the same time, Miss Johnson urged aggressiveness on her candidate.

"Don't back down," she implored. "Remember the policeman!"

Mrs. Carrington muttered maliciously, as she caught the words.

"In view of Mrs. Flynn's record," she began, "I scarcely feel justified—" Her mock humility was copied by Mrs. Flynn on the instant.

"As a stranger, I cannot force myself—"

The presiding officer decided that this was in truth the psychological moment in which to dominate the situation.

"Indeed, the chair appreciates the rare quality of your self-denial," she announced in an authoritative voice that commanded the respectful attention of all. "Now, ladies," she continued with an air of grave rebuke, "you see what comes of putting your hostess in such an unfortunate position as compelling her to force on one of her guests something she doesn't want. Mrs. Carrington and Mrs. Flynn, both, are my friends and my guests as well, and I must certainly decline to embarrass them further in this matter. The only thing I can do, since neither of them is willing to take the presidency, is regretfully to accept it myself. So, I will be president, and I do now so declare myself."

At this astounding decision, Mrs. Carrington and Mrs. Flynn sank down in their chairs, too dumfounded to protest: but their distress, along with the similar emotion of Mrs. Morton and Miss Johnson, was not observed by the others in the general hubbub of enthusiasm aroused by the new Solomon come to judgment. After an interval of tumultuous cheering, there came demand for a speech by the newly fleeted president.... Cicily acceded, after due urging.

"I'm ever so much obliged to you," she declared, and kissed her hands gracefully to her fellow club-members. Thereat, the applause was of the briskest. "Really, I am," she made assurance, and wafted another kiss. On this occasion, the applause was of even greater volume than ever before, although four of those present did not join in the ovation to the new chief executive. "Yes, really—truly!" Cicily went on, fluently. "And I think this is a wonderful club we have started. We need a club. It gives us—us married women—something to do. That's the real answer—the real cause, I think, of the woman question. These men have gone on inventing vacuum cleaners and gas-stoves and apartment hotels and servants that know more than we do. They haven't treated us fairly. They've taken away all our occupation, and now we've got to retaliate. We can't keep house for them any more, and, if we—if we care anything about them, or want to help them, we've got to go into business, or to help them vote.... Well, they brought it on themselves. They've got too proud. They used to be dependent on us: now, we're dependent on them, on their inventions and their servants. So, we're going to show them. We'll make them dependent on us in the wider outside world, just as they used to be dependent on us in the home. They've hurt our pride, and we're going to make them pay. They say we are nervous and reckless and always on the go.... It's their fault: they've made the new woman, and now we are going to make the new man. They put us out of work, and made us so, and now they're going to be sorry.... The time is fast coming when each of us will have at least three or four men—"

It was Miss Johnson who caused the interruption to this burst of eloquence.

"Why, that's positively immoral!" gasped the outraged spinster.

"—at least three or four men dependent upon her," concluded the unabashed president of the Civitas Club, as she cast a withering look on her enemy, who quailed visibly. "And I think that's all," Cicily added, contentedly. She felt that she could with justice claim to have conducted herself nobly throughout a critical situation.

"I move that we adjourn," said Mrs. Flynn, energetically. Her vigorous temperament would permit no longer sulking in silence despite the humiliation to which she had so recently been subjected.

Mrs. Carrington, however, had not yet rejected all hope of office.

"We must first select a secretary," she suggested.

This was opposed by Miss Johnson, always persistently moved to discredit the older woman who had snubbed her socially.

"Why not select a professional stenographer as a member of the club; then make her secretary? Any number of young working women would doubtless be glad of the honor." This brought an outcry against the admission of any professional working woman into the exclusive Civitas.

"Oh, remember that we have ideals!" Ruth Howard remonstrated, with sincere, if vague, adherence to her ideals; and she up-turned her great eyes toward the ceiling.

Mrs. Flynn, curiously enough, was opposed to the idealist in this instance.

"Yes," she said, "I fear that it's quite true. The professional working woman thinks more of her salary and a comfortable living than of our great cause."

Cicily herself disposed of the matter with a blithesome nonchalance that was beautiful to behold.

"Oh, don't bother," was her way of cutting the Gordian knot. "I'll make my husband's stenographer do the work."

"I move that we adjourn," the militant suffragette repeated in a most businesslike manner.

Mrs. Carrington was determined that her rival should not outdistance her at the finish. She spoke with her most forcible dignity:

"I second the motion."

The motion was put and carried.... Thus ended the first session of that epoch-marking organization: The Civitas Society for the Uplift of Woman and for Encouraging the Spread of Social Equality among the Masses.

CHAPTER II

Cicily Hamilton, bride of a year, was seemingly as fortunate a young woman as the city of New York could offer to an envious world. Her house in the East Sixties, just off the Avenue, was a charming home, dainty, luxurious, in the best of taste, with a certain individuality in its arrangement and ornamentation that spoke agreeably of the personality of its mistress. Her husband, Charles Hamilton, was a handsome man of twenty-six, who adored his wife, although recently, in the months since the waning of the honeymoon, he had been so absorbed in business cares that he had rather neglected those acts of tenderness so vital to a woman's happiness. Some difficulties that disturbed him downtown rendered him often preoccupied when at home, and the effect on his wife was unwholesome. Little by little, the girl-woman felt a certain discontent growing within her, indeterminate in a great measure, but none the less forceful in its influence on her moods day by day.

The statements that Cicily had made in her inaugural speech to the Civitas Society exhibited, albeit crudely, some of the facts breeding revolt in her. In very truth, she found herself without sufficient occupation to hold her thoughts from fanciful flights that led to no satisfactory result in action. An excellent housekeeper, who was far wiser in matters of ménage than she could ever be, held admirable sway over the domestic machinery. The servants, thus directed, were as those untroubling inventions of which she had complained. Since she was not devoted to the distraction of social gaieties, Cicily found an appalling amount, of unemployed time on her hands. She was blest with an excellent education; but, with no great fondness for knowledge as such, she was not inclined to prosecute any particular study with the ardor of the scholar. To rid herself of the boredom induced by this state of affairs, the young wife decided that she must develop a new interest in her fellow creatures. She went farther, and resolved to establish herself on a basis of equality with her husband, not merely in love, but in the sterner world of business. Thus, she was brought to entertain a convincing belief in equality for the sexes, in society and in the home.

She revealed something of her mind and heart to her aunt on the afternoon of the day following the singular session of the Civitas Society. The two women were together in Cicily's boudoir, a delightful room, all paneled in rose silk, with furniture *Louis Quatorze*, and Dresden ornaments.... It was an hour yet before time for the dressing-bell. Cicily, in a negligee of white silk that fitted well with the color scheme of the room and that only emphasized the purity of her ivory skin, suddenly sat up erect in the chair where she had been nestling in curving abandonment.

"Why, Aunt Emma," she exclaimed, with a new sparkle in the amber eyes, "we forgot to set any date for another meeting of the club?"

But Mrs. Delancy did not seem impressed by the oversight.

"Do you think it makes any real difference, dear?" she questioned placidly.

At this taunt, Cicily assumed an air of reproach that was hardly calculated to deceive the astute old lady, who had known the girl for twenty years.

"Don't you take our club seriously?" she questioned in her turn. Her musical voice was touchingly plaintive.

"Oh, it's serious enough," was the retort. "It's either seriously pitiful, or pitifully serious, whichever way you choose to look at it."

Cicily abandoned her disguise of concern, and laughed heartily before she spoke again.

"I must admit that I think it's a joke, myself," she admitted: "more's the pity." There was a note of genuine regret in her voice now. Then, she smiled again, with much zest. "But it was so amusing—stirring them up, and then calmly taking the presidency myself, because none of them knew just how to stop me!"

"It was barefaced robbery!" Mrs. Delancy exclaimed reprovingly, although she, too, was compelled to smile at the audacity of the achievement. "But," she added meditatively, "I really don't see what it all amounts to, anyhow?"

"I suspect that you didn't listen attentively to the president's speech," Cicily railed.

"I listened," Mrs. Delancy declared, firmly. "In spite of that fact, my dear, what does it all mean? Down deep, are you serious in some things I have heard you say, lately?"

"Oh, yes, I'm serious enough," was the answer, spoken with a hint of bitterness in the tone. "That is, I'm seriously bored—desperately bored, for the matter of that. I tell you, Aunt Emma, a married woman must have something to do. As for me, why, I have absolutely nothing to do. Those other women, too, or at least most of them, have nothing to do, and they are all desperately bored. Well, that's the cause of the new club. Unfortunately, the club, too, has nothing to do—nothing at all—and so, the club, too, is desperately bored.... Oh, if only I could give that club an object—a real object!"

Mrs. Delancy murmured some remonstrance over the new enthusiasm that sounded in her niece's voice while uttering the aspiration in behalf of the Civitas Society; but the bride paid no heed.

"Yes," she mused, straightening the arches of her brows in a frown of perplexity, "it could be made something, with an object. I myself could be made something, with an object—something worth while to strive for.... Heavens, how I wish I had something to do!"

This iconoclastic fashion of speech was not patiently endured by the orthodox aunt, who listened to the plaint with marked displeasure.

"A bride with a young husband and a beautiful home," she remarked tartly, "seeking something to do! In my day, a bride was about the busiest and the happiest person in the community." Her voice took on a tone of tender reminiscence, and a little color crept into the wrinkled pallor of her cheeks, and she perked her head a bit coquettishly, in a youthful manner not unbecoming, as she continued: "I remember how happy—oh, how happy!—I was then!"

Cicily, however, displayed a rather shocking lack of sympathy for this emotion on the part of her relative. She was, in fact, selfishly absorbed in her own concerns, after the manner of human nature, whether young or old.

"Yes," she said, almost spitefully, "I have noticed how always old married ladies continually remember the happy time when they were brides. A bride's happy time is as much advertised as a successful soap.... But I—I—well, I'm not a bride any longer—that's all. I've been married a whole year!"

"A whole year!" Mrs. Delancy spoke the word with the fine scorn of one who was looking forward complacently to the celebration of a golden wedding anniversary in the near future.

Cicily, however, was impervious to the sarcasm of the repetition.

"Yes," she repeated gloomily, "a whole year. Think of it.... And all the women in my family live to be seventy. Mamma would have been alive if she hadn't been drowned. A good many live to be eighty. Why, you're not seventy yet. Poor dear! You may have ten or a dozen more years of it!"

Mrs. Delancy was actually horrified by her niece's commiseration.

"Cicily," she eluded, "you must not speak in that manner. I've been happily married. You—"

The afflicted bride was not to be turned aside from her woe.

"I'm perfectly wretched," she announced, fiercely. "Auntie, Charles is a bigamist!"

"Good Lord!" Mrs. Delancy ejaculated with pious fervor, and sank back limply in her chair, too much overcome for further utterance. Then, in a flash of memory, she beheld again the facts as she had known them as to her niece's courtship and marriage. The girl and Charles Hamilton had been sweethearts as children. The boy had developed into the man without ever apparently wavering in his one allegiance. Cicily, too, had had eyes for no other suitor, even when many flocked about her, drawn by the fascination of her vivacious beauty and the little graces of her form and the varied brilliance of her moods. It was because of the steadfastness of the two lovers in their devotion that Mr. and Mrs. Delancy had permitted themselves to be persuaded into granting consent for an early marriage. It had seemed to them that the constancy of the pair was sufficiently established. They believed that here was indeed material for the making of an ideal union. Their belief seemed justified by the facts in the outcome, for bride and groom showed all the evidences of rapturous happiness in their union. It had only been revealed during this present visit to the household by the aunt that, somehow, things were not as they should be between these two erstwhile so fond.... And now, at last, the truth was revealed in all its revolting nudity. Mrs. Delancy recalled, with new understanding of its fatal significance, the aloof manner recently worn by the young husband in his home. So, this was the ghastly explanation of the change: The man was a bigamist! The distraught woman had hardly ears for the words her niece was speaking.

"Yes," Cicily said, after a long, mournful pause, "besides me, Charles has married—" She paused, one foot in a dainty satin slipper beating angrily on the white fur of the rug.

"What woman?" Mrs. Delancy demanded, with wrathful curiosity.

"Oh, a factory full of them!" The young wife spoke the accusation with a world of bitterness in her voice.

"Good gracious, what an extraordinary man!" Mrs. Delancy, under the stimulus of this outrageous guilt again sat erect in her chair. Once more, the flush showed daintily in the withered cheeks; but, now, there was no hint of tenderness in the rose—it was the red of anger. "I know how you must feel, dear," she said, gently. "I was jealous once, of one woman. But to be jealous of a factory full—oh, Lord!"

"Yes," Cicily declared, in tremulous tones, "all of them, and the men besides!"

Mrs. Delancy bounced from her seat, then slowly subsided into the depths of the easy chair, whence she fairly gaped at her former ward. When, finally, she spoke, it was slowly, with full conviction.

"Cicily, you're crazy!"

"No," the girl protested, sadly; "only heartbroken. I am so miserable that I wish I were dead!"

"But, my dear," Mrs. Delancy argued, "it can't be that you are quite—er—sensible, you know."

"Of course, I'm not sensible," Cicily admitted, petulantly. "I said I was jealous, didn't I? Naturally, I can't be sensible."

"But Charles can't be married to the men, too!" Mrs. Delancy asserted, wonderingly.

At that, Cicily flared in a burst of genuine anger.

"Yes, he is, too," she stormed; "and to the women, too—to the buildings, to the machinery, to the nasty ground, to the fire-escapes—to every single thing about that horrid business of his! Oh, I hate it! I hate it! I hate every one of them!... And he is a bigamist, I tell you—yes, a bigamist! He's married to me and to his business, too, and he cares more for his business!"

"Humph!" The exclamation came from Mrs. Delancy with much energy. It was surcharged, with relief, for the tragedy was made clear to her at last. Surely, there was room for trouble in the situation, but nothing like that over which she had shuddered during the period of her misapprehension. In the first minute of relief, she felt aroused to indignation against her niece who had so needlessly shocked her. "I do wish, Cicily," she remonstrated, "that you would endeavor to curb your impetuosity. It leads you into such absurdities of speech and of action. Your extravagant way of opening this subject caused me utterly to mistake your meaning, and set me all a-tremble—for a tempest in a teapot."

"I think I'll get a divorce," Cicily declared, defiantly. The bride was not in an apologetic mood, inasmuch, as she regarded herself as the one undeservedly suffering under great wrongs.

"Perhaps!" Mrs. Delancy retorted, sarcastically. Her usual good humor was returning, after the first reaction from the stress she had undergone by reason of the young wife's fantastic mode of speech. "I suppose you will name Charles's business as the co-respondent."

"It takes more out of him than any woman could," was the spirited retort. "Of course, I shall. Why not?"

Mrs. Delancy, now thoroughly amused, explained to her niece some details concerning the grounds required by the statutes in the state of New York for the granting of absolute divorce, of which hitherto the carefully nurtured girl had been in total ignorance. Cicily was at first astounded, and then dismayed.

But, in the end, she regained her poise, and reverted with earnestness to the need of reform in the courts where such gross injustice could be. She surmised even that in this field she might find ultimately some outlet of a satisfactory sort for her wasted energies.

"Why, I and my club, and other clubs like it," she concluded, "find the cause of our being in such things as this. We women haven't any occupation, and we haven't any husbands, essentially speaking—and we're determined to have both."

The bold declaration was offensive to the old lady's sense of propriety.

"You can't interfere with your husband's business, Cicily," she said by way of rebuke, somewhat stiffly.

The young wife, however, was emancipated from such admonitions. She did not hesitate to express her dissent boldly.

"Yes," she exclaimed indignantly, "that's the idea that you old married women have been putting up with, without ever whimpering. Why, you've even been preaching it yourselves—preaching it until you've spoilt the men utterly. So, now, thanks to your namby-pamby knuckling under always, it's business first, last, and all the time—and marriage just nowhere. I tell you, it's all wrong.... I know you're older," she went on vehemently, as Mrs. Delancy's lips parted. "I guess that's why you're wrong.... Anyhow, it isn't as it was intended. For the matter of that, which was first, marriage or business? Did Adam have a business when he married? Huh! There! No man could answer that!" Cicily paused in triumph, and, in the elation wrought by developing a successful argument, turned luminous eyes on her aunt, while her red lips bent into the daintiest of smiles.

Mrs. Delancy was not to be beguiled from the fixed habits of thoughts carried through scores of years by the winsome blandishments of her whilom ward. She had no answering gentleness for the gladness in the girl's face. When she spoke, it was with an emphasis of acute disapproval:

"Do you mean that you are going to make your husband choose between you and his business, Cicily?"

Something in the tone disturbed the young wife's serenity. The direct question itself was sufficient to destroy the momentary equanimity evolved out of a mental achievement such as the argument from Adam. She realized, on the instant, that her desire must be defeated by the facts of life.

"No," she admitted, after a brief period of hesitancy, "of course not. Charles chooses business first—any man would."

The inexorable question followed:

"Well, what are you going to do?" Then, as no answer came: "I beg of you, Cicily, not to be rash. Don't do anything that will cause you regret after you have come into a calmer mood. Of course, once on a time, marriage was first with men, and I think that it should be first now—I know that it should. But it is the truth that business has now come to be first in the lives of our American men. And, my dear, you can't overcome conditions all by yourself. At heart, Charles loves you, Cicily. I'm sure of that, even though he does seem, wrapt up in his business affairs. Yet, he loves you, just the same. That's the one thing we older women learn to cling to, to solace ourselves with: that, deep down in their hearts, our husbands do love us, no matter how indifferent they may seem. When a woman once loses faith in that, why, she just can't go on, that's all. Oh, I beg you, Cicily, don't ever lose that faith. It means shipwreck!"

The young wife shook her head slowly—doubtfully; then quickly—determinedly.

"No, I won't put up with just that," she asserted, morosely, "I want more. I'll have more, or—" She checked herself abruptly, and once again the arch of her dark brows was straightened, as she mused somberly over her future course.

There fell an interval of silence, in which the two reflected on the mysteries that lie between man and woman in the way of love. It was broken finally by Mrs. Delancy, who spoke meditatively, hardly conscious that the words were uttered aloud.

"Of course, you're not really dependent on Charles. Your own fortune—"

The girl's interruption came in a passionate outburst that filled her hearer with distress and surprise. It would seem that Cicily had been thinking very tenderly, yet very unhappily, of those mysteries of love.

"But I am dependent on him—dependent on him for every ray of sunshine in my heart, for every breath of happiness in my life; while he—" her voice broke suddenly; it came muffled as she continued quiveringly—"while he—he's not dependent on me at all!" After a little interval, she went on, more firmly, but with the voice of despair. "That's the pity of it. That's what makes us women nowadays turn to something else—to some other man, or to some work, some fad, some hobby, some folly, some madness—anything to fill the void in our hearts that our husbands forget to fill, because their whole attention is concentrated on business.... But I'm not going to be that wife, I give you warning. I'm going to make my husband fill all my heart, and, too, I'm going to make him dependent on me. I'll make him know that he can't do without me!"

"Nonsense!" Mrs. Delancy objected, incredulously. "Why, as to that, Charles is dependent on you now. You haven't really lost his love—not a bit of it, my dear!"

There was infinite sadness in the young wife's gesture of negation.

"Aunt Emma," she said earnestly, "Charles and I haven't had an evening together in weeks. We haven't had a real old talk in months.... Why, I—I doubt if he even remembers what day this is!"

"You mean—?"

"Our first anniversary! Long ago, we planned to celebrate the day—just the theater and a little supper after—only us two.... I wonder if he will remember." The tremulous voice gave evidence that the tears were very near.

"Oh, of course, he will," Mrs. Delancy declared briskly, with a manner of cheerful certainty. Nevertheless, out of the years of experience in the world of married folk, a great doubt lurked in her heart.

Cicily's head with the coronal of dark brown hair, usually poised so proudly, now drooped dejectedly; there was no hopefulness in her tones as she replied:

"I don't know—I am afraid. Why, since the tobacco trust bought out that Carrington box factory five months ago, and began fighting Charles, he talks tobacco boxes in his sleep."

"Don't take it so seriously," the aunt argued. "All men are that way. My dear, your Uncle Jim mumbles woolens—even during Dog Days. No, you mustn't take things so seriously, Cicily. You are not the only wife who has to suffer in this way. You are not the only one who was ever lonesome. Your case isn't unusual—more pity! It's the case of almost every wife whose husband wins in this frightful battle with business. Years ago, dear, I suffered as you are suffering. Your uncle never told me anything. I've never known anything at all about more than half of his life. He rebuffed me the few times at first, when I tried to share those things with him. He said that a woman had no place in a man's business affairs. So, after a little, I stopped trying. For a time, I was lonesome—very lonesome—oh, so lonesome!... And, then, I began to make a life for myself outside the home—as he had already by his business. I tried in my humble way to do something for others. That's the best way to down a heartache, my dear—try making someone else happy."

The words arrested Cicily's heed. As their meaning seeped into her consciousness, the expression of her face changed little by little. "Making people happy!" She repeated the phrase as she had formulated the idea again, very softly, with a persistence that would have surprised Mrs. Delancy, could she have caught the inaudible murmur. Presently, the faint rose in the pallor of her cheeks blossomed to a deeper red, and the amber eyes grew radiant, as she lifted the long, curving lashes, and fixed her gaze on her aunt. There was a new animation in her voice as she spoke; there was a new determination in the resolute set of the scarlet lips.

"Why, that's something to do!" she exclaimed, joyously. "It's something to do, really, after all—isn't it?"

"Yes," her aunt agreed, sedately; "something big to do. For my part, I joined church circles, and worked first for the heathen."

"Oh, bother the heathen!" Cicily ejaculated, rudely. "Charles is heathen enough for me!" With her characteristic impulsiveness, she sprang to her feet, as Mrs. Delancy quietly rose to go, ran to her aunt, and embraced that astonished woman with great fervor.

"I honestly believe that you've given me the idea I was looking for," she declared enthusiastically. "You darling!... Making people happy! It would be something for the club, too.... Yes," she concluded decisively, "I'll do it!"

"Do what?" Mrs. Delancy questioned, bewildered by the swift succession of moods in the girl she loved, yet could never quite understand.

"You just wait, Aunt Emma," was the baffling answer.

Mrs. Delancy turned at the door, and spoke grimly:

"My dear Cicily," she said, "you're getting to be quite as reticent as your uncle and Charles."

But the girl disdained any retort to the gibe. Instead, she was saying softly, over and over: "Making other people happy! Making other people happy!"

CHAPTER III

Cicily Hamilton was inclined to be captious with her maid as she dressed that evening. She was finical to the point of absurdity even, which is often the fault of beauty, and perhaps a fault not altogether unbecoming, since its aim is the last elaboration of loveliness. Indeed, the fault becomes a virtue, when its motive lies in the desire to attain supreme charm for the one beloved. It was so with the young wife to-night. She was filled with anxious longing to display her beauty in its full measure for the pleasuring of the man to whom she had given her whole heart. For that fond purpose, she was curt with her maid, and reproachful with herself. She was deeply troubled by the thought that a darker shade to her brows might enhance the brilliance of her eyes. She hesitated before, but finally resisted, a temptation to use a touch of pencil to gain the effect. She was exceedingly querulous over the coiling of her tresses into the crown that added so regally to the dignity of her bearing. The selection of the gown was a matter for profound deliberation, and ended in a mood of dubiety. That passed, however, when at last she surveyed her length in the cheval glass. Then, she became aware, beyond peradventure of doubt, that the white lacery of silk, molded to her slender form and interwoven with heavy threads of gold, was supremely becoming. The gleam of precious metal in the fabric scorned to transmute the amber of her eyes into a glory of gold. The pearls of her necklace harmonized with the warm pallor of her complexion.

Despite the pains taken, there remained time to spare before the dinner hour, when the toilette had been thus happily completed. As she was about to dismiss the maid, Cicily bethought her to ask a question.

"Has Mr. Hamilton come in yet, Albine?"

"Yes, madam—a half-hour ago. He went to the study, with his secretary."

Left alone, Cicily mused on the maid's information, and bitterness again swept over her. During the period of dressing, she had been so absorbed in the attempt to make the most of her charms that, for the time being, she had forgotten her apprehensions as to her husband's neglect. Now, however, those apprehensions were recalled, and they became more poignant. Only a stern regard for the appearance she must present anon held her back from tears. It seemed to her longing a dreadful thing that on this day of all others her husband must bring back to his home this rival of whom she was so jealous. For it could mean nothing else, if he were closeted with his secretary at this hour: he was dallying in the embraces of business, with never a thought for the wife whom he had sworn to love always. For all that she was beautiful, possessed of ample fortune, married to the man of her choice and, by reason of her youth, full of the joy of life, Cicily Hamilton was a very wretched woman, as she strolled slowly down the broad, winding stair, and entered the drawing-room, where already Mrs. Delancy was waiting.

That good lady, in her turn, had found herself sorely perturbed. The mood of revolt in which her niece was, caused a measure of alarm in the bosom of the loving older woman. Her own course at this moment was not clear to her. She had been aware that to-day was the first anniversary of the marriage of the Hamiltons, and it was on this account that she had prolonged her visit. Yet, she had meant to go away in time to permit the young pair their particular fête in a *solitude à deux*. She, too, however, had learned of the present absorption of Mr. Hamilton in business affairs, and there at she became suspicious that her niece's fears as to his forgetfulness might be realized. In the end, she had determined to remain until immediately before the dinner hour, leaving the going or staying to be ruled by the facts as they developed. Arrived at this decision, she had telephoned to her own home as to the uncertainty in regard to her movements, and thereafter had awaited the issue of events with that simple placidity which is the boon sometimes granted by much experience of the world.

Hardly a moment after the meeting of the two women in the drawing-room, the master of the house entered hurriedly, bearing in his hand a sheaf of papers. Charles Hamilton was a large, dark man, remarkably good-looking in a boyish, clean-shaven, typically American, businesslike fashion. Still short of the thirties, he had nevertheless formed those habits of urgent industry that characterize the successful in the metropolis. Already, he had become enslaved by the business man's worst habit—that most dangerous to domestic happiness—the taking of mutual love between him and his wife as something conceded once for all, not requiring exhibition or culture or protection or nourishment of any sort. In this mistake he was perhaps less blamable than are some, inasmuch as he was fettered by a great ignorance of feminine nature. From earliest boyhood, he had been Cicily's abject worshiper. That devotion had held him aloof from other women. In consequence, he had missed the variety of experiences through which many men pass, from which, perforce, they garner stores of wisdom, to be used for good or ill as may be. Hamilton, unfortunately, knew nothing concerning woman's foibles. He had no least suspicion as to her constant craving for the expression of affection, her heart-hunger for the murmured words of endearment, her poignant yearning for gentle, tender caresses day by day. They loved; they were safely married: those blessed facts to him were sufficient. There was no need to talk about it. In fact, in his estimation, there was not time. There was business to be managed—no dillydallying in this day and generation, unless one would join the down-and-out club! Such was the point of view from which this bridegroom of a year surveyed his domestic life. It was a point of view established almost of necessity from the environment in which he found himself established. He was in no wise unique: he was typical of his class. He was clean and wholesome, industrious, energetic, clever—but he knew nothing of woman.... So, now, he immediately rushed up to Mrs. Delancy, without so much as a glance toward the wife who had studied long and anxiously to make the delight of his eyes.

"Hello, Aunt Emma!" he exclaimed gaily, and kissed her. "I am glad you stayed over to cheer up the little girl, while husband was away grubbing the money for her."

"Oh, do you think, then, that she needs cheering?" There was a world of significance in the manner with which the old lady put the pertinent question; but the absorbed business man was deaf to the implication.

Cicily, however, spared him the pains of any disclaimer by uttering one for herself.

"Need cheering!—I! What an absurd idea!"

Hamilton smiled gladly as he heard his wife speak thus bravely in assurance of her entire contentment. Now, for the first time, he turned toward her. But it was plain that he failed to note her appearance with any degree of particularity. He had no phrase of appreciation for the exquisite woman, in the exquisite gown. He spoke with a certain tone of fondness; yet it was the fondness of habit.

"That's right," he said heartily, as he crossed the room to her side, and bestowed a perfunctory marital peck on the oval cheek. "I'm mighty glad you haven't been lonesome, sweetheart."

"You were thinking that I might be lonesome?" There was a note of wistfulness in the musical voice as she asked the question. The glow in the golden eyes uplifted to his held a shy hint of hope.

Manlike, he failed to understand the subtle appeal.

"Of course, I didn't," he replied. "If I thought about it at all—which I greatly doubt, we've been so rushed at the office—I probably thought how glad you must be not having a man under foot around the house when your friends called for gossip. Oh, I understand the sex; I know how you women sit about and talk scandal."

An indignant humph! from Mrs. Delancy was ignored by Hamilton, but he could not escape feeling a suggestion of sarcasm in his wife's deliberately uttered comment:

"Yes, Charles, you do know an awful lot about women!"

"I knew enough to get you," he riposted, neatly. Then, he had an inspiration that he believed to be his duty as a host: as a matter of fact, it was rudeness in a husband toward his wife on the first anniversary of their marriage. He turned suavely to Mrs. Delancy. "You'll stay to dinner, of course, Aunt Emma." And he added, fatuously: "You and Cicily can chat together afterward, you know.... I've a horrible pile of work to get through to-night."

At her husband's unconscious betrayal of her dearest hopes, Cicily started as if she had been struck. As he ceased speaking, she nerved herself to the ordeal, and made her statement with an air as casual as she could muster, while secretly a-quiver with anxiety.

"Why, Charles, we are going to the theater to-night, you know."

"To-night?" Hamilton spoke the single word with an air of blank astonishment. It needed no more to make clear the fact that he had no guess as to the importance of this especial day in the calendar of their wedded lives.

Cicily's spirits sank to the lowest deeps of discouragement before this confession of her husband's inadvertence to that which she regarded as of vital import in the scheme of happiness.

"Yes," she answered dully, "to-night. I have the the tickets. Don't you remember what day this is?" She strove to make her tone one of the most casual inquiry, but the attempt was miserably futile before the urge of her emotion.

"Why, to-day is Thursday, of course," Hamilton declared, with an ingenuous nonchalance that was maddening to the distraught wife.

"Yes, it is Thursday," she rejoined; and now there was no mistaking the bitter feeling that welled in the words. "It is the anniversary of our wedding day."

Hamilton caught his unhappy bride in his arms. He was all contrition in this first moment when his delinquency was brought home to consciousness. He kissed her tenderly on the brow.

"By Jove, I'm awfully sorry, dear." There was genuine regret for such culpable carelessness in his voice. "How ever did I forget it?" He drew her closer in his embrace for a brief caress. Then, after a little, his natural buoyancy reasserted itself, and he spoke with a mischievousness that would, he hoped, serve to stimulate the neglected bride toward cheerfulness. "I say," he demanded, "did you remember it all by yourself, sweetheart, or did Aunt Emma remind you? I know she's a great sharp on all the family dates."

The badinage seemed in the worst possible taste to the watching Mrs. Delancy, but she forbore comment, although she saw her niece wince visibly. Cicily's pride, however, came to her rescue, and she contrived to restrain herself from any revelation of her hurt that could make itself perceptible to Hamilton, who now released her from his arms.

"Oh," she said with an assumption of lightness, "Aunt Emma told me, of course. How in the world could you suppose that I, in my busy life, could possibly remember a little thing like the anniversary of our wedding?"

"No, naturally you wouldn't," the husband agreed, in all seriousness. "Gad! If you hadn't been so engrossed with that wonderful club and all your busy society doings, you probably would have remembered, and then you would have told me."

The young wife perceived that it would be impossible to arouse him to any just realization of the flagrancy of his fault. Yet, she dared venture a forlorn hope that all was not yet lost.

"Well, anyhow, Charles," she said, very gently, "I have got the tickets, and it is our anniversary."

"Even if I had remembered about it," was the answer, spoken with a quickly assumed air of abstraction, as business returned to his thoughts, "I couldn't have gone to-night. You see, I have a conference on—very important. It means a great deal. Morton and Carrington are coming around to see me.... I can't bother you with details, but you know it must be important. I can't get out of it, anyhow."

"But, Charles—" The voice was very tender, very persuasive. It moved Hamilton to contrition. The pleading accents could never have been resisted by any lover; but by a husband—ah, there is a tremendous difference, as most wives learn. Hamilton merely elaborated his defense against yielding to his wife's wishes.

"I tell you, Cicily, it's a matter of business—business of the biggest importance to me. You're my wife, dear: you don't want to interfere with my business, do you? Why, I'll leave it to Aunt Emma here, if I'm not right." He faced about toward Mrs. Delancy, with an air of triumphant appeal. "Come, Aunt Emma, what would you and Uncle Jim do in such a case?"

"I think Cicily already knows the answer to that question," was the neutral reply, with which Hamilton was wholly satisfied.

Now, indeed, the girl abandoned her last faint hope. The magnitude of the failure shook her to the deeps of her being. She felt her muscles relax, even as her spirit seemed to grow limp within her. She was in an agony of fear lest she collapse there under the eyes of the man who had so spurned her adoration. Under the spur of that fear, she moved forward a little way toward the window, the while Hamilton chatted on amiably with Mrs. Delancy, continuing to justify the position he had taken. As he paused finally, Cicily had regained sufficient self-control to speak in a voice that told him nothing beyond the bare significance of the words themselves.

"Oh, of course, you're right, Charles. Don't bother any more about it. Attend to your conference, and be happy. There will be plenty more anniversaries!"

CHAPTER IV

The preliminary conference with Morton and Carrington, which had so fatally interfered with Cicily's anniversary plans, proved totally unsatisfactory from the standpoint of Charles Hamilton. As a matter of fact, a crisis had arisen in his business affairs. He was threatened with disaster, and as yet he was unable to see clearly any way out. He was one of countless individuals marked for a tidbit to glut the gormandizing of a trust. He had by no means turned craven as yet; he was resolved to hold fast to his business until the last possible moment, but he could not blind himself to the fact that his ultimate yielding seemed inevitable.

In circumstances such as these, it was natural enough that Hamilton should appear more than ever distrait in his own home, for he found himself wholly unable to cast out of his mind the cares that harassed him. They were ever present during his waking moments; they pursued him in the hours devoted to slumber: his nights were a riot of financial nightmares. He was polite to his wife, and even loverlike with the set phrases and gestures and caresses of habit. Beyond that, he paid her no attention at all. His consuming interest left no room for tender concerns. He had no time for social recreations, for the theater, or functions, or informal visits to friends in Cicily's company. His dark face grew gloomy as the days passed. The faint creases between the eyebrows deepened into something that gave warning of an habitual frown not far away in the future, which would mar the boyish handsomeness of his face. The firm jaw had advanced a trifle, set in a steadfast defiance against the fate that menaced. His speech was brusquer.

Cicily, already in a state of revolt against the conditions of her life, was stimulated to carry out the ideas nebulously forming in her alert brain. She felt that the present manner of living must soon prove unendurable to her. It was essential that a change should be made, and that speedily, for she was aware of the limitations to her own patience. Her temperament was not one to let her sit down in sackcloth and ashes to weep over the ruins of romance. Rather, she would bestir herself to create a new sphere of activity, wherein she might find happiness in some other guise. Yet, despite the ingenuity of her mind, she could not for some time determine on the precise course of procedure that should promise success to her aspirations. Primarily, her desire was to work out some alteration in the status of all concerned by which the domestic ideal might be maintained in all its splendid integrity. But her tentative efforts in this direction, made lightly in order that their purport might not be guessed by the husband, were destined to ignominious failure. Mrs. Delancy, a week after the melancholy anniversary occasion, made mention of the fact that she had cautiously spoken to Charles in reference to his neglect of the young wife. She explained that his manner of reply convinced her that, in reality, the man was merely a bit too deeply occupied for the moment, and that, when the temporary pressure had passed, everything would again be idyllic. Mrs. Delancy's motive in telling her niece of the interview was to convince this depressed person that the matter was, after all, of only trifling importance. In this, however, she failed signally. Cicily regarded the incident as yet another evidence of a developing situation that must be checked quickly, or never. But she took advantage of the circumstances to introduce the topic with Hamilton. To her, the conversation was momentous, although neither by word nor by manner did she let her husband suspect that the discussion was aught beyond the casual.

As usual now, Hamilton, on his return at night from the office, had shut himself in the library, and was busily poring over a bundle of papers, when there came a timid knock at the door. In response to his call, Cicily entered. The young man greeted his wife politely enough, and even called her "darling" in a meaningless tone of voice; but the frown did not relax, and constantly his eyes wandered to the bundle of documents. Cicily, however, was not to be daunted, for his manner was no worse than she had expected. She crossed to a chair that faced his, and seated herself. When, finally, she spoke, it was with an air of tender solicitude, and the smile on her scarlet lips was gently maternal.

"You are working too hard, dear," she remonstrated. "You must relax a little when you are away from the office, or you'll have—oh, brain-fag, or nervous prostration, or some such dreadful thing."

"Well, I'll try to put the office out of my head for a little while," was the obedient answer, which gave the woman the chance she desired.

"But you must do it for your own sake—not mine, you know. You see, Aunt Emma told me that she had been lecturing you a bit—said you ought to pay me more attention, and all that sort of thing."

"Yes, and so I shall; but I'm pressed to death just now—After a bit—"

"You are so different!" Cicily said, almost timidly, as his voice trailed into silence. "Sometimes, I think—I fear—" Her voice, in turn, died.

For the moment, the husband was moved to a sudden tenderness. He spoke softly, earnestly, leaning toward her.

"Cicily, you can't realize what a pleasure it is to a fellow, when he is pounding away downtown, to stop for a second and think of his wife at home waiting for him—that dear girl who loves him—the darling one far away from all the turmoil of the sordid fight."

The rhapsody, although genuine enough, was not satisfying to the wife. The limit of time to a "second" was unfortunate. There was distinct irony in her tone as she answered with a question:

"And the farther away the home, the greater the pleasure, doubtless?"

For once, Hamilton was susceptible; and he was keenly distressed, momentarily.

"Cicily!" he cried. "You don't doubt my love, do you? Why, when a man and a woman marry, each ought to take the other's love for granted—take it on faith."

But the wife was in no wise consoled by this trite defense. It had been made too familiar to her in previous discussions between them. Her answer was tinged with bitterness:

"That's the only way in which I've had a chance to take it lately," she said slowly, with her eyes downcast.

The persistence of her mood aggravated the man beyond the bounds of that restraint which he had imposed on himself. His nerves were overwrought, and, under the impulse of irritation over another worry at home added to those by which he was already overburdened, he flared.

"Cicily!" he exclaimed, sharply. "What in the world has come over you? You don't want to hold me back, do you? You don't want to be that sort of a wife?"

"Charles!" Cicily exclaimed, in her turn sharply. She was grievously hurt by this rebuke from the man whom she loved.

"Forgive me!" Hamilton begged, swiftly contrite. "I'm just nervous—tired. It's been a fearfully hard day downtown."

His obvious sincerity won instant forgiveness. Cicily rose from her chair, and came to seat herself on the arm of his. He took one of her hands in his, and her free hand stroked his hair in a familiar caress. When she spoke, it was with a tenderness that was half-humility.

"Would it help, dear, to talk to me? We used always to talk over things, you know. Don't you remember? You said ever so many times that I had so much common sense!"

Again, Hamilton spoke with a tactlessness that was fairly appalling:

"Oh, yes, I remember very well. That was before we were married."

"Yes—before!" There was scorn in the emphasis of the repetition. It aroused the husband to knowledge of his blunder.

"I—didn't mean to—" he stammered. "I—I—of course, you understand—Really, dearest, I'm sorry I've been so occupied lately. I hope things will brighten up soon; then, I shall be more sociable. I've thought about our anniversary, too. It's too bad I was tied up that night!"

Cicily rose from her position on the arm of her husband's chair, and strolled across the room.

"Oh, that's all right," she remarked, in an indifferent tone of voice. "Of course, business must come first." Her beautiful face was very somber now; her eyes were turned away from the man.

But Hamilton was amply content. His absorption in other things rendered him somewhat unobservant of certain niceties in expression just now. He sprang up, and went to his wife. With his hands on her shoulders, he declared his satisfaction with the situation as it appeared to him at this time:

"That's my real Cicily—my little girl!... Now, another anniversary—"

"Oh, yes," the wife agreed, "as I reminded you before, there will be plenty of other anniversaries—lots more—so many more!" The melancholy note in her voice escaped the listener, as she had known that it would. His answer was enthusiastic:

"Yes, indeed! Both of our families are long-lived. Do you remember, when we got engaged, how you said it was so awfully serious, because all the women in your family lived to be seventy or more?"

"Yes, I remember!" Then, abruptly recalling the original motive with which she had sought this conversation, Cicily, by an effort of will that cost her much, spoke with a manner half-gaily sympathetic:

"Charles, why don't you tell me now all about this horrid business of yours?"

At the question, the man's face quickly grew grim, and the frown deepened perceptibly between his brows. He dropped his hands from his wife's shoulders, turned away, and went back to reseat himself in the chair by the broad table, on which was spread out the bundle of business papers. He did not look up toward the woman, who followed him with something of timidity, and took her position anew in the chair facing him. He had no eyes for the pleading anxiety in the gaze that was fixed on him. His mood was once more heavy under the weight of business worry.

"Oh, what's the use of telling you!" he snapped, brutally; but that he had meant nothing personal in the question was shown at once, for he added, in the same sentence: "—or anybody else?"

Cicily had whitened a little at the opening phrase, but her color crept back, as she heard the end of the impatient question. After a little, she ventured to repeat her request for some information as to the status of affairs in the factory.

"Why, as to that," Hamilton replied, in a tone of discomfort, "the facts are simple enough; but they spell disaster for me, unless I can contrive some way or another out of the mess in which I'm involved by the new moves. You see, Carrington has sold his factory. He's sold out to the trust—that's the root of the whole trouble. So, he and Morton are making a fight against me. They mean to put me down and out. It's good business from their standpoint; but it's ruin for me, if they succeed. They think that I'm only a youngster, and that I sha'n't be able to stand up against their schemes. They are of the opinion that, since Dad is gone, they will have a snap in wiping me off the map. They fancy that I don't know a blessed thing in the world except football." Hamilton paused for a moment, and his jaw shot out a little farther forward; his lips shut tensely for a few seconds. Then, they relaxed again, as he continued his explanation of the situation that confronted him. "They're down in my territory now, plotting to undermine my business in various ways. They have the belief that I am not up to their plans; but I know more than they give me credit for." His voice rose a little, and grew harsher. "Well, I'm not such a fool as they fancy I am, perhaps. I'm going to show 'em! I'm in this game, and I'm going to fight, and to fight hard. I'm not going to let 'em score. The play won't be over till the whistle blows. I tell you, I'll show 'em!"

As he continued speaking, the wife's expression changed rapidly. By the time he had come to a pause, it was radiant. Indeed, now, for the first time in many dreary weeks, Cicily felt that she was truly a wife in all senses of the word. Here, at last, she was become a helpmeet to her husband. That *bête noire* business was no longer the thing apart from her. She was made the confidante of her husband's affairs abroad. She was made the recipient of the most vital explanations. She was asked to share his worries, to counsel him. Thus, in her usual impulsiveness, the volatile girl was carried much too far, much beyond the actuality. As Hamilton ceased speaking, she leaned forward eagerly. The rose was deeply red in her cheeks; the amber eyes were glowing. Her voice was musically shrill, as she cried out, with irrepressible enthusiasm:

"Yes, yes, Charles, we'll show 'em! We'll show 'em!"

For a moment, the man stared at the speaker dumfounded by the unexpected outbreak. Presently, however, the import of her speech began to be made clear to him. "We?" he repeated, doubtfully. "You mean—" He hesitated, then added: "You mean that you—and I—that is, you mean that you—?"

"Yes, yes," Cicily answered hastily, with no abatement of her excitement and triumph. "Yes, together, we'll show 'em!"

At this explicit declaration, Hamilton burst out laughing.

"You!" he ejaculated, derisively.

"Yes, I," Cicily maintained, stoutly. "Why, I showed Mrs. Carrington the other day. Next, we'll beat her husband. You know, I beat her for the presidency of the club."

"Well, then, stick to your club, my dear," Hamilton counseled, tersely. "I'll attend to the real business for this family." His face was grown somber again.

"That's just like Uncle Jim," Cicily retorted, bitterly disappointed by this disillusionment. "I suppose you want me to be like Aunt Emma."

"She's perfect—certainly!"

Cicily abandoned the struggle for the time being, acknowledging almost complete defeat. There was only a single consoling thought. At least, he had talked with her intimately concerning his affairs. With an abrupt change of manner, she stood up listlessly, and spoke in such a fashion as might become an old-fashioned wife, although her voice was lifeless.

"I'll get your house-coat, dear," she said, simply. "And, then, while you look after your business during the evening, I'll do—my knitting!" Her hands clenched tightly as she went forth from the study, but the master of the house was unobservant when it came to such insignificant details. He was already poring over the documents on the table; but he called out amiably as he heard the door open.

"That's the dear girl!" he said.

CHAPTER V

Two evenings after this memorable interview between husband and wife, Carrington and Morton were closeted with Hamilton in his library. To anyone who had chanced to look in on the group, it would have seemed rather an agreeable trio of friends passing a sociable evening of elegant leisure. Hamilton alone, as he sat in the chair before the table, displayed something of his inner feelings by the creases between his brows and the compression of his lips and a slight tensity in his attitude. Morton was stretched gracefully in a chair facing that of his host and prospective victim, while Carrington was close by, so that the two seemed ranked against the one. A close student of types would have had no hesitation in declaring Morton to be much the more intelligent and crafty of the two visitors. He appeared the familiar shrewd, smooth, well-groomed New Yorker, excellently preserved for all his sixty-five years; one who could be at will persuasive and genial, or hard as steel. In his evening dress, he showed to advantage, and his manner toward Hamilton was gently paternal, as that of an old family friend who has chanced in for a pleasant hour with the son of a former intimate. Carrington, on the contrary, was of the grosser type of successful business man. A frock-coat sufficed him for the evening always. There was about him in every way a heaviness that indicated he could not be a leader, only a follower after the commands of wiser men. But, in such following, he would be of powerful executive ability.

"Do you know," Morton was saying, "it's really a great personal pleasure for me to come here, Hamilton, my boy. It reminds me of the many times when I used to sit here with your father." As he ceased speaking, he smiled benevolently on the young man opposite him.

Hamilton nodded, without much appearance of graciousness. He was more than suspicious as to the sincerity of this man's kindly manner.

"Yes, I know," he said. "You and he had many dealings together, I believe, didn't you, Mr. Morton?"

"Oh, yes, indeed," came the ready answer; "many and many. He was a shrewd trader, was your father. It's a pity he cannot be here to know what a promising young man of business his son has become. He would be proud of you, my boy."

"Thank you, Mr. Morton," Hamilton responded. "For that matter, I myself wish that Dad were here just now to help me."

Again, the visitor smiled, and with a warm expansiveness that was meant to indicate a heart full of generous helpfulness.

"You don't need him, my boy," he declared, unctuously. "You are dealing with an old friend."

Carrington nodded in ponderous corroboration of the statement.

"Of course not, of course not!" he rumbled, in a husky bass voice.

Hamilton let irritation run away with discretion. He spoke with something that was very like a sneer:

"I thought possibly that was just why I might need him."

Morton seemed not to hear the caustic comment. At any rate, he blandly ignored it, as he turned to address Carrington.

"You remember Hamilton, senior, don't you?" he asked.

"Very well!" replied the gentleman of weight. His red face grew almost apoplectic, and the big body writhed in the chair. His tones were surcharged with a bitterness that he tried in vain to conceal. Morton regarded these signs of feeling with an amusement that he had no reluctance in displaying. On the contrary, he laughed aloud in his associate's face.

"Well, yes," he said, still smiling, "I fancy that you ought to remember Hamilton, senior, and remember him very well, too. But, anyhow, by-gones are by-gones. You weren't alone in your misery, Carrington. He beat me, too, several times."

Hamilton smiled now, but wryly.

"So," he suggested whimsically, yet bitterly, "now that he's dead, you two gentlemen have decided to combine in order to beat his son. That's about it, eh?"

Carrington, who was not blessed with a self-control, or an art of hypocrisy equal to that of his ally, emitted a cackling laugh of triumph. But Morton refused to accept the charge. Instead, he spoke with an admirable conviction in his voice, a hint of indignant, pained remonstrance.

"Ridiculous, my dear boy—ridiculous! Just look on me as being In your father's place. No, no, Hamilton, there's room for all of us. There's a reasonable profit for all of us in the business—if only we'll be sensible about it."

"It only remains to decide as to the sensible course, then," Hamilton rejoined, coldly. "I suppose, in this instance, it means that I should decide to follow the course you have outlined for me. Now, I have your offer before me on this paper. Briefly stated, your proposition to me is that you will take all the boxes I am able to deliver to you—that is to say, you agree to keep my factory busy. For this promise on your part, you require two stipulations from me as conditions. The first is that I shall not sell any boxes to the Independent Plug Tobacco Factory; the second is that I shall sell my boxes to you at a regular price of eleven cents each. I believe I have stated the matter accurately. Have I not?"

"You have stated it exactly," Morton assured the questioner. "That is the situation in a nutshell."

"Unfortunately," Hamilton went on, speaking with great precision, "it's quite impossible for me to make any such agreement with you—utterly impossible." He looked his adversary squarely in the eye, and shook his head in emphatic negation.

Carrington merely emitted a bourdon grunt. Morton, however, maintained the argument, undeterred by the finality of Hamilton's manner.

"But, my dear boy," he exclaimed quickly, "we're not asking you to do anything that you haven't done already. Why, you furnished me with one lot at nine cents."

"At a loss, in order to secure custom against competition," was the prompt retort. "It costs exactly eleven cents to turn out those boxes."

Morton persisted in his refusal to admit the justice of the young man's refusal to accept the terms offered.

"But, my dear boy," he continued, "take your last four bids. I mean the bids that you and Carrington made before we bought out Carrington. The first, time, Carrington bid eleven cents; while you bid fourteen. On the second lot Carrington bid thirteen; and you bid nine."

"You illustrate my contention very well," Hamilton interrupted. "At eleven cents a box, Carrington hardly quit even. It was for that reason he bid thirteen on the following lot; while I, because I was bound to get a look in on the business, even at a loss—why, I bid nine cents. The result was that I got the order, and it cost me a loss of just two cents on each and every box to fill it." A contented rumble from the large man emphasized the truth of the statement.

Nothing daunted, Morton resumed his narrative of operations in the box trade.

"On the third lot, Carrington bid eight cents, while you bid eighteen."

Carrington's indignation was too much for reticence.

"Yes, I got that order," he roared, wrathfully. "It was a million box order, too—" The withering look bestowed on the speaker by Morton caused him to break off and to cower as abjectly in his chair as was possible to one of his bulk.

"His success in being the winner in that bout cost him three cents each for the million boxes," Hamilton commented. "Well?"

"Well," Morton said crisply, "for the fourth and biggest order, Carrington bid seventeen, and you bid sixteen."

"Yes, yes!" Carrington spluttered, forgetful of the rebuke just administered to him. "And, on the four lots, Hamilton, you cleaned up a profit, while I lost out—so much that I had to sell control of my plant. And you call that fair competition!"

Morton grinned appreciation. The young man regarded the ponderous figure of Carrington with something approaching stupefaction over the sheer bravado of the question.

"Was that your motive in joining the trust," he demanded ironically: "to get fair competition?"

Again, Morton laughed aloud, in keen enjoyment of the thrust.

"You're your own father's son, Hamilton," he declared, gaily.

Hamilton, however, was not to be cajoled into friendliness by superficial compliment.

"Probably," he said sternly, "I might not have been able to do so well, if you had not been clever enough to let both Carrington and myself each see the figures of the other's secret bid as a great personal favor."

As the words entered Carrington's consciousness, the ungainly form sat erect with a sudden violence of movement that sent the chair sliding back three feet over the polished floor. The red face darkened to a perilous purple, and the narrow, dull eyes flashed fire. He struggled gaspingly for a moment to speak—in vain. Morton's eyes were fixed on the man, and those eyes were very clear and very cold. Carrington met the steady stare, and it sobered his wrath in a measure, so that presently he was able to utter words intelligibly. But, now, they were not what they would have been a few seconds earlier:

"You—you told him what I bid?"

Hamilton took the answer on himself.

"Surely, he did, Carrington." The young man spoke with cheerfulness, in the presence of the discomfiture of his enemy. "He told you what I bid; and, in just the same way, he told me what you bid—every time!"

For a long minute, Morton stared on at his underling whom he had betrayed. Under that look, the unhappy victim of a superior's wiles, sat uneasily at first, in a vague effort toward defiance; then, his courage oozed away, he shifted uneasily in his seat, and his eyes wandered abashedly about the room. Convinced that the revolt was suppressed, Morton turned again to the young man opposite him.

"All that is done with now." The tone was sharp; the mask of urbanity had fallen from the resolute face, which showed now an expression relentless, dominant. "Hamilton, what are you going to do?" The manner of the question was a challenge.

"I can't make money selling boxes at eleven cents," Hamilton answered wearily. "Nobody could."

"At least, you won't lose any," was the meaning answer. Then, in reply to Hamilton's half-contemptuous shrug, Morton continued frankly. "After all, Hamilton, you can make a profit. It won't be large, but it will be a profit. This is the day of small profits, you must remember. It will be necessary for you to put in a few more of the latest-model machines, and to cut labor a bit. In that way, you will secure a profit. You must cut expense to the limit."

The young man regarded Morton with strong dislike.

"What you mean," he said angrily, "is that I must put my factory on a starvation business. Now, I don't want to cut wages. It's a sad fact that the men at present don't get a cent more than they're worth. Besides that, some of them have been working in the factory for father more than thirty years."

"There is no room for such pensioners in these days of small profits," Morton declared, superciliously. "However, it's no business of mine. Remember, though, it's your only chance to keep clear."

"No," Hamilton announced bravely, "I'll not cut the wage-scale. I'll sell to the trade, at thirteen. It's mighty little profit, but it's something."

Morton shook his head.

"The Carrington factory," he said threateningly, "will sell to the trade for ten cents, until—"

"—Until I'm cleaned out!" Hamilton cried, fiercely.

Morton lifted a restraining hand. He was again his most suave self.

"My dear boy," he said gently, "I liked your father, and I esteemed him highly. He was a shrewd trader: he never tried to match pennies against hundred-dollar bills.... The moral is obvious, when you consider your factory alone as opposed to certain other interests. So, take my advice. Try cutting. The men would much rather have smaller wages than none at all, I'm sure. Think it over. Let me know by Saturday.... The Carrington factory is to issue its price-list on Monday."

Hamilton was worn out by the unequal combat. He hesitated for a little, then spoke moodily:

"Very well. I'll let you know by Saturday."

When, at last, his guests had departed, the wretched young man dropped his head on his arms over the heap of papers, and groaned aloud.... He could see no ray of hope—none!

CHAPTER VI

It was a half-hour after the breaking up of the conference when Hamilton at last raised his head from his arms. He looked about him dazedly for a little while, as if endeavoring to put himself in touch once again with the humdrum facts of existence. Then, when his brain cleared from the lethargy imposed by the strain to which it had so recently been subjected, he gave a sudden defiant toss of his head, and muttered wrathfully: "Go broke, or starve your men!" He got out of his chair, and paced to and fro swiftly for a little interval, pondering wildly. But, of a sudden, he reseated himself, drew a pad of paper to him, and began scrawling figures at the full speed of his pencil. And, as he wrote, he was murmuring to himself: "There is a way out—there must be!"

It was while the husband was thus occupied that the door opened softly, without any preliminary knock, and the wife stepped noiselessly into the room. The anxiety that beset her was painfully apparent in her bearing and in the expression of her face. Her form seemed drooping, as if under shrinking apprehension of some blow about to fall. The eyes of amber, usually so deep and radiant, were dulled now, as if by many tears; the rich scarlet of the lips' curves was bent downward mournfully. She stood just within the doorway for a brief space, watching intently the man who was so busy over his scrawled figures. At last, she ventured forward, walking in a laggard, rhythmic step, as do church dignitaries and choir-boys in a processional. By such slow stages, she came to a place opposite her husband. There, she remained, upright, mute, waiting. The magnetism of her presence penetrated to him by subtle degrees.... He looked up at her, with no recognition in his eyes.

"They've gone, dear?" She spoke the words very softly, for she understood instinctively something as to the trance in which he was held.

Hamilton's abstraction was dissipated as the familiar music of Cicily's voice beat gently on his ears.

"Yes—oh, yes, they've gone." His voice was colorless. His eyes went out to the array of figures that sprawled recklessly over the sheet before him.

But the young woman was not to be frustrated in her intention by such indifference on his part. She spoke again, at once, a little more loudly:

"Tell me: Did you come out all right?"

Hamilton raised his head with an impatient movement. Evidently, this persistence was a distracting influence—a displeasing. There was harshness in his voice as he replied:

"Did I come out all right? Well, yes—since I came out at all. Oh, yes!" His voice mounted in the scale, under the impulse of a sudden access of rage against his enemies. He spoke with a savage rapidity of utterance: "And I can lick Carrington any day in the week. Why, I've already put him out. It's Morton—that old fox Morton who's got me guessing.... What do you think? They even had the nerve to threaten me. Of course, it was in a round-about way; but it was a threat all the same. They threatened to close up the Hamilton factory. Gad! the nerve of it!"

"They threatened to close up your factory, Charles?" Cicily exclaimed, astonished and angry. "But you own the Hamilton factory. What have they to do with it? The impudence of them!"

"Yes, I own the factory, all right," the husband agreed. "But, you see—" Hamilton broke off abruptly, and was silent for a moment. When he spoke again, the liveliness was gone from his voice: it was become quietly patronizing. "Oh, let's forget it, dear. I must be going dotty. I'll be talking business with you, the first thing I know."

"I only wish you would!" Cicily answered, with a note of pleading in her tones.

"Nonsense!" was the gruff exclamation. "The idea of talking business with you. That would be a joke, wouldn't it?" He spoke banteringly, with no perception of the gravity in his wife's desire to share in this phase of his life. But he looked up from the papers after a moment into his wife's face. She had turned from him, and then had reclined wearily in the chair opposite him, whence she had been staring at him with a tormenting feeling of impotence. The expression on her face was such that Hamilton realized her distress, without having any clue to its cause.

"Now, sweetheart, what's wrong?" he questioned. He was half-sympathetic over her apparent misery, half-annoyed.

Cicily, with the intuitive sensitiveness of a woman to recognize a lover's hostile feeling beneath the spoken words, was acutely conscious of the annoyance; she ignored the modicum of sympathy. To conceal her hurt, she had resort to a fictitious gaiety that was ill calculated, however, to deceive, for the stress of her disappointment was very great.

"The matter with me?" she repeated, with an assumption of surprise. "Why, the matter with me is that I'm so happy—that's all!"

"Cicily!" Now, at last, the husband was both shocked and grieved over his wife's mood.

"Yes, that's it—happy!" the suffering girl repeated. "Why, I'm so happy—just so happy—that I could scream!"

Hamilton leaned forward in his chair, to regard his wife scrutinizingly. He was filled with alarm over the nervous, almost hysterical, condition in which he now beheld her.

"Cicily, are you well?" he asked. There was a distinct quaver of fear in his voice. "You look—strange, somehow."

"Oh, not at all!" came the flippant retort. "It's merely that you haven't really taken a good look at me lately—until just this minute. So, of course, I'd look a bit strange to you."

It must be remembered that Hamilton, although usually intelligent, had a clear conscience and no suspicion whatsoever as to any culpability on his part in his relations with his wife: thus it was that now he was wholly impervious to the sarcasm of her reference, which he answered with the utmost seriousness.

"My dear, I saw you this morning, last night—oh, heaps of times, every day."

"Oh, your physical eyes have seen; but your mind, your heart, your soul—the true you—hasn't seen me for I don't know how long."

This cryptic explanation was too subtle for Hamilton to grasp while yet his brain was fogged by the intricacies of his business affairs. He gazed on his wife in puzzled fashion for a few seconds, then abandoned the problem as one altogether beyond his solving. To clear up a vague suspicion that this might be some new astonishing display of a woman's indirect wiles, he put a question:

"My dear, do you want a new automobile, or a doctor?"

"Neither!" came the crisp reply; and for once the musical voice was almost harsh, "I want a husband!"

"Good Lord! Another?" Hamilton was pained and scandalized, as, indeed, was but natural before a confession so indecorous seemingly and so unflattering to himself.

"I don't want the one I have now," Cicily affirmed, with great emphasis. She rather enjoyed the manner in which the man shrank under her declaration. But he said nothing as she paused: he was momentarily too dumfounded for speech, "I want my first one back," Cicily concluded.

Hamilton gaped at his wife, powerless to do aught beyond grope in mental blackness for some ray of understanding as to this horrible revelation made by the woman he loved.

"You—you want your first one back!" he repeated stupidly, at last. Of a sudden, a gust of fury shook him. "God!" he cried savagely. "And I thought I knew that girl!"

Cicily rested unperturbed before the outbreak. She was absorbed in her own torment, with no sentiment to spare for the temporary anguish she was inflicting on her husband, which, in her opinion, he richly deserved.

"You did know me once," she answered, coldly. "That was before you changed toward me."

The injustice of this charge, as he deemed it, was beyond Hamilton's powers of endurance. He sprung from his chair, and stood glowering down on Cicily, who bore the stern accusation of his eyes without flinching. The pallor of her face was a little more pronounced than usual, less touched from within with the hue of abounding health, and her crimson mouth was less tender than it was wont to be. But she leaned back in her chair in a posture of grace that displayed to advantage the slender, curving charm of her body, and her eyes, shining golden in the soft light of the room, met the man's steadfastly, fearlessly.

"I—changed—to you!" Hamilton stormed. "Cicily! Cicily! What madness! You know—oh, absurd! Why, Cicily, I love you.... I think of you always!"

"Oh, yes, you love me," Cicily agreed, contemptuously, "You think of me always—when your other love will let you."

"Cicily!"

"I mean it," came uncompromisingly, in answer to Hamilton's look of horror. "I mean every word of it!"

"Cicily," the husband besought, as a great dread fell on his soul, "remember, you are my wife—my love!"

"Yes, I'm one of them." The tone was icy; the gaze fixed on his face was unwavering.

But this utterance was too sinister to be borne. The pride of the man in his own faithfulness was outraged. His voice was low when he spoke again, yet in it was a quality that the young wife had never heard before. It frightened her sorely, although she concealed its effect by a mighty effort of will.

"That is an insult to you and to me, Cicily. It is an insult I cannot—I will not—permit."

It was evident to Cicily that she had carried the war in this direction far enough; she hastened her retreat.

"Oh, I didn't say that you were in love with another woman," she explained, with an excellent affectation of carelessness. "For that matter, I know very well that you're not." Then, as Hamilton regarded her with a face blankly uncomprehending, she went on rapidly, with something of the venomous in her voice: "Sometimes, I wish you were. Then, I'd fight her, and beat her. It would give me something to do." She paused for a moment, and laughed bitterly. "Oh, please, Charles, do fall in love with some other woman, won't you?"

Hamilton started toward the telephone in the hall.

"It's the doctor you want, not the automobile," he called over his shoulder.

"Nonsense!" Cicily cried. "Stop!" And, as he turned back reluctantly, she went on with her explanation: "No, it isn't the lure of some siren in a Paquin dress—or undress: it's the lure of the game—the great, horrid, hideous business game, which has got you, just as it's got most of the American husbands who are worth having. That's the lure we American women can't overcome; that's the rival who is breaking our hearts. You are the man of business, Charles—I'm the woman out of a job! That's all there is to it."

Hamilton listened dazedly to this fluent discourse, the meaning of which was not altogether clear to him. He frowned in bewilderment, as he again seated himself in the chair opposite his wife. He could think of nothing with which to rebuke her diatribe, save the stock platitudes of a past generation, and to these necessarily he had immediate recourse.

"You have the home—the house—to look out for, Cicily. That's a woman's work. What more can you wish?"

"The home! The house!" The exclamation was eloquent of disgust. "Ah, yes, once on a time, it was a woman's work—once on a time! But, then, you men were dependent on us. Marriage was a real partnership. Nowadays, what with servants and countless inventions, so that machinery supplies the work, the home is a joke. The house itself is an automatic machine that runs on—buttons, push-buttons. You men can get along without us just as well. You don't really depend on us for anything in the home. Your lives are full up with interest; every second is occupied. Our lives are empty. My life is empty, Charles. I'm lonely, and heart-hungry, I've no ambition to go in for bridge. I'm not a gambler by choice. I don't wish to follow society as a vocation. I'm not eager even to be a suffragette. I want to be an old-fashioned wife—to do something that counts in my husband's life. I want him to depend on me for some things, always. I want to be my husband's partner." Little by little, while she was speaking, the coldness passed from the woman's voice; in its stead grew warmth; there was passionate fervor in the final plea. It moved Hamilton to pity, although he was ignorant as to the means by which he might assuage his wife's so great discontent. Manlike, he attempted to overcome emotion by argument.

"Cicily," he urged, "just now, I'm up to my ears and over in work. They are crowding me mighty hard. There's dissatisfaction at the mill—danger of a strike. Morton is heading a syndicate—a trust, really—trying to absorb us. I'm fighting for my very life—my business life.... Cicily, you wouldn't throw obstacles in my way now, would you?"

"Obstacles! No; I want to help you."

"In business?" Hamilton queried, astounded. "You—help me—in business?"

"Yes," Cicily answered, steadily. "I can do something, I know." There was intensity of purpose in the glow of the golden eyes, as they met those of her husband; there was intensity of conviction in the tones of her voice as she uttered the assurance. She realized that the crisis of her ambition was very near at hand.

"You can do nothing." The man's blunt statement was uttered with a conviction as uncompromising as her own. The egotism of it repelled the woman. There was a hint of menace in her manner, as she replied:

"Take care, Charles. Don't shut me out. You're making a plaything of me— not a wife.... And I—I won't be your plaything!"

"You mean—?"

"I mean," went on the wife relentlessly, "that this is the most serious moment of our married life. If you put me off now, if you shut me out of your life now—out of your full life—I can't answer for what will happen."

There followed a long interval of silence, the while husband and wife stared each into the other's eyes. In these moments of poignant emotion, the profound feeling of the woman penetrated the being of the man, readied his heart, and touched it to sympathy—more: it mounted to his brain, which it stimulated to some measure of understanding. That understanding was fleeting enough, it was vague and incomplete, as must always be man's inadequate knowledge of woman. But it was dominant for the time being. Under its sway, Hamilton spoke in gracious yielding, almost gratefully.

"Very well. You can help."

The young wife sat silent for a time, thrilling with the joy of conquest. The roses of her cheeks blossomed again; the radiance of her eyes grew tender; the scarlet lips wreathed in their happiest curves. At last, she rose swiftly, and seated herself on the arm of her husband's chair. She wound her arms about his neck, and kissed him fondly on cheek and brow and mouth.

Hamilton accepted these caresses with the pleasure of a fond bridegroom of a year, and, too, with a certain complacency as the tribute of gratitude to his generosity. But, when she separated herself again from his embrace, he was moved to ask a question that was calculated to be somewhat disconcerting.

"What can you do?" he demanded.

"Oh, I don't know," Cicily answered, nonchalantly; "but something. I shall do something big! You see, you've done so much. Now, I must do something too—something big!"

"But what have I done?" the husband questioned, perplexed anew by this charming wife of many moods.

"What have you done?" Cicily repeated, joyously. "Why, you've made me the happiest woman in the world—a partner!" Again, the rounded arms were wreathed about his neck; her face was hidden on his shoulder.

Hamilton's eyes were turned ceilingward, as if seeking some illumination from beyond. He listened, stupid, bemused, to that word echoing wildly through his brain: "Partner!" He understood fully at last, and with understanding came utter dismay. "Partner!... Oh, Lord!"

CHAPTER VII

In the days that followed, Cicily was almost riotously happy. The schemes that had been formulating themselves dimly in her mind following the altruistic suggestion made to her by Mrs. Delancy now took on definite shape and became substantial. In view of the fact that her husband had explicitly brought her into a business partnership with himself, it occurred to her that she might well combine the idea of making other people happy with practical uses in behalf of business. To this end, then, she devoted her intelligence diligently, with the result that she soon had concrete plans of betterment for the many, and these of a sort to redound directly to her husband's advantage in a business way. In brief, she conceived certain philanthropic operations to be carried out for the enjoyment of her husband's employés; the effect of such changes would inevitably be a better understanding between them and their employer, and an increased loyalty and efficiency on the part of the workers. With this laudable purpose, Cicily, after broaching the subject in detail to Hamilton, who made no objection, since her helpfulness was to be operated out of her private fortune, at once busied herself with the execution of the project. The factory downtown was soon a-chatter with excitement over the startling innovations that were under way. The employés cursed or cheered according to their natures, as they learned of the gifts bestowed by the wife of their employer. They regarded the new bath-tubs with wonder, albeit somewhat doubtfully. They discussed the library with appreciation, or lack of appreciation, according to their degrees of illiteracy or learning: the socialistic element condemned the inanity of the volumes selected; there were only histories, biographies, books of travel, foolish novels and the like— nothing to teach the manner by which the brotherhood of man must be worked out.

In addition to her activities for good in this direction, Cicily added something actual to her ideas in reference to the up-lift of woman. She made herself known to the wives of some of the men who worked in the factory, and called on them in their homes. She invited them to visit her in return, and she matured a project to make the Civitas Society her ally in this noble work of up-lift and equalization in the social order. With such eager works, her days were filled full, and she was glad in the realization that it was, indeed, become her splendid privilege to share in her husband's broader life.... She was his—partner!

It may be doubted if Hamilton had more than the shadow of knowledge as to his wife's happiness in the changed order. The episode, as he deemed it, in which she had been given a partnership with him, hardly remained in his memory. When he thought of it at all, he smiled over it as over the vagary of one among a woman's innumerable varying moods. But he thought of it very rarely, for his time was absorbed in the desperate struggle to find a way out from the destruction that loomed very close at hand. In the end, he decided not to reject the offer made by Morton in behalf of the trust. Otherwise, he would be confronted by Carrington's competition in selling to the independent trade at a dead loss. But he was determined ultimately to combat this competition to the limit of his ability and capital. It was apparent to him that success would be impossible from the outset unless he should reduce his operating expenses to the minimum. For this reason, he planned to make the cut in wage-scale that had been suggested by Morton, although in reality it was to overcome the machinations of the trust, not to further them. He solaced his conscience by reiteration of the truth: that, in the event of winning, the reduction would have been but a temporary thing; whereas, without it, he must close down the factory immediately. For the sake of his workers, as well as for his own, he was resolved to pursue the one course that offered a hope of victory.

Naturally enough, the employés did not understand or approve. When news of the proposed cut in the scale was made known, there came clamor and wrath and sorrow. Meetings of the workers were held, and in due time a committee of three waited on Hamilton by appointment in the study of his house uptown. Schmidt, the most garrulous of the three, was a man in the prime of life, heavily built, bald, with a white mustache that gave him a certain grotesque resemblance to Bismarck. The other two members of the committee were Ferguson, a thin, alert-mannered Yankee of forty, who spoke with a pronounced drawl; and McMahon, a short, red-headed, shrewd Irishman, with a face on which shone a volatile good-humor. The three, on entering the library and being greeted by Hamilton, found that their employer had fortified himself for the conference by the presence of Mr. Delancy, in whose business judgment the younger man had great confidence. The men received the pleasant salutation of Hamilton with awkwardness, but without any trace of shamefacedness, for they had the consciousness of their righteous cause to give them confidence in a strange environment. Hardly were they seated at their host's request in chairs facing him and Mr. Delancy, when Schmidt bounced up, and, after squaring himself resolutely in a position of advantage before the empty fireplace, proceeded to declaim vigorously as to the rights between labor and capital, speaking sonorously, with a pronounced German accent. After some five minutes of this, Mr. Delancy, who was both nervous and irritable, as the orator paused for breath at a period, ventured to protest.

"Yes, yes, man," he exclaimed, testily. "But I don't care a damn about Schopenhauer and socialism, and I'm sure Mr. Hamilton doesn't. Let's get to the wages paid in the Hamilton factory."

Ferguson came to the support of Delancy, as did McMahon, who said amiably:

"Give the boss a chance, Smitty."

Schmidt, however, was inclined to be recalcitrant.

"There was no arrangement yet to give the boss a chance," he argued.

"Just give him a chance then because he's a friend of mine," urged the Irishman with a grin of such exceeding friendliness toward the German himself that it was not to be resisted. Schmidt nodded in token that the employer should be allowed to speak, but he retained his position as a presiding officer before the fireplace.

Hamilton forthwith set out to present his side of the case to the men before him.

"As you know," he said briskly, "I'm the owner of the Hamilton factory. I pay the wages. Now, the Hamilton factory has been kept running through good times and through bad times for more than thirty years. Sometimes, too, it has been run at a loss, without any cut in the wage-scale to help the owner in that period of loss. Well, it seems to me under the circumstances that I have a right to run my own business."

"Oh, certainly!" Ferguson agreed, languidly.

But Schmidt added a correction to the general concession.

"As long as you run it in our way, and don't cut wages."

"I'm sorry, men," Hamilton retorted, without any avoidance of the issue; "but that cut must go."

The members of the committee looked from one to another, and shook their heads dolefully. They knew too well the hardships that would be wrought among their fellows by a ten per cent. cut the length of the scale. It was McMahon who spoke first, with his usual air of good-nature in the sarcasm, but a note of grimness underlying the surface pleasantry.

"Well, now, you see," he said in his rich brogue, addressing Ferguson and Schmidt, "the boss has to save a mite to pay for the new bath-tubs and that natty bit of a gymnasium and the library they've been putting in lately."

"*Ach, Himmel!*" Schmidt snorted, disgustedly. "We will have manicures soon already!" He stared at his pudgy fingers with the work-begrimed nails, and grinned sardonically.

Hamilton flushed under the taunts.

"I have nothing to do with those improvements," he declared, in self-justification. "They are all being put in by Mrs. Hamilton at her own expense. She is doing it to make you men and women there more contented with your lot—to make you happy."

"To make us happy!" Schmidt grunted. "Bathtubs!"

McMahon's sense of humor led him to indulge in another flight of pleasantry, which shadowed forth the grim reality of these lives.

"Sure, but the gymnasium is great," he said, blandly. His tone was so deceptive that Hamilton smiled in appreciation of the compliment to his wife's undertaking, and even Mr. Delancy relaxed the harsh set of his features. "The longer you work in it," the Irishman continued innocently, "outside of hours of course, the stronger you get, and the more you can do in hours for the boss.... Sure, it's great!"

Hamilton hastily changed the subject. He explained that, the cut would not be applied to the wages of the women in the packing-department, where a hundred were employed. He declared frankly that their pay was insufficient to stand such a reduction.

"And do you think we make enough to stand it?" Ferguson exclaimed, indignantly.

"Somebody has to stand it," was Hamilton's moody retort. "You have threatened to strike, if I make this cut. Well, I am forced to threaten you in turn. If you won't accept the cut, I shall strike—I must strike!"

Schmidt, from his position before the fireplace, rose on his toes in high indignation.

"You strike!" he clamored, huffily. "Who has given you that permission to strike? You are no union. Bah!"

Hamilton shrugged his shoulders, wearily.

"Listen, men," he requested. "I'll put the facts before you plainly, for I place my whole confidence in your loyalty. You think, perhaps, that you're being strung in this deal. Well, we'll all be strung, and hung over the side of the boat, too, unless we work together. You men are dissatisfied, because, although you are working full time, you are asked to take a ten per cent. cut. The truth of the matter is that the factory is not making a cent of profit. I have to make the boxes for sale at a loss now, on account of the competition of the trust factory, which is trying to put me out of business. I must work at cost, or even at a loss, for a time. With the ten per cent. cut, I can keep going. Without it, I must close down. As soon as this crisis is over, if I win out, the old wage-scale will be restored. I hope that time will not be long away. I may venture to tell you something in confidence: I'm planning to take on some side lines—some things in which I hope to make big money. As soon as they're started, I'll give you back the present scale."

"Why don't your wife help pay the wages?" Schmidt questioned, shrewdly. "She has plenty of money for foolishness."

"Faith, and that isn't a bad idea at all, at all, Mr. Hamilton," McMahon agreed. "It's a better use for her money. Since she's been coming around to the house these last few weeks, it's cost me a week's pay to get a hat for my old woman in imitation of hers.... Women have no place in business, I'm thinking."

Ferguson added his testimony to the like effect:

"That's right," he declared. He looked about for a place in which to spit by way of emphasis, but, seeing none, forbore. "My girl, Sadie, she put two dollars in false hair this very week. Your wife is sure making it mighty hard for us, Mr. Hamilton. How can I buy false hair with a ten per cent. cut? Durned if I can see!"

Again, Hamilton was afflicted with embarrassment over the infelicitous results of his wife's benevolent activity, and again he changed the subject.

"Well, boys," he said frankly, "I've put the matter to you straight. I'm sorry. But, unless you take the cut, I don't see any future for any of us.... It's up to you."

"The men decide for themselves," Ferguson replied, glumly. "We only report back to them."

"But you three really decide," Hamilton persisted. "Come, give me your decision now."

Ferguson and McMahon regarded each other doubtfully, in silence, as if uncertain how to proceed. But Schmidt was not given to hesitation in expressing himself on any occasion. He spoke now with an air of phlegmatic determination, brandishing his right arm at the start:

"Well, speaking for myself only, I want to say—How do you do, Mrs. Hamilton."

CHAPTER VIII

As Schmidt concluded his oratorical flourish in this astonishing fashion, the other occupants of the room turned amazedly, to behold Cicily herself, standing in the open doorway of the study.

The young wife was a very charming, radiant vision, as she rested there motionless. She was gowned for the street, wearing that ravishing hat which had been the cause of McMahon's undoing, a dainty and rather elaborate device in black and red, and a black cloth gown, short and closely cut, which showed to delightful advantage the lissome curves of her form. Beneath, a luxurious *chaussure* in black showed the inimitable grace of tiny feet and ankles. Now, as she regarded the company in some astonishment, the perfect oval of her cheeks was broken by the play of dimples as she smiled a general welcome on the men before her. But her attention was particularly arrested by Schmidt, who, after his first greeting in words, was now bowing stiffly from the hips, a feat of some difficulty by reason of his girth. Cicily watched the formal performance with mingled emotions of amusement and alarm. When, at last, it was successfully accomplished, however, and the pudgy figure straightened, she recognized the socialist, and came forward.

"Why, it's Mr. Schmidt!" she exclaimed, cordially. "I'm so glad to see you!" To this, the German murmured a guttural response, too much overcome by pleasure for coherent speech. The new-comer passed on, and made her greetings to Ferguson and McMahon with the like pleasant hospitality, shaking hands with each.

"This is, indeed, charming," she exclaimed heartily. "Did you bring your wives along?"

Schmidt, as usual, constituted himself the spokesman.

"Mrs. Hamilton," he stated, with somber impressiveness, "this is business."

"Good gracious!" Mrs. Hamilton exclaimed, with some trepidation. "I hope it's nothing that they would not approve of."

"Be easy," Ferguson, admonished, soothingly. "Sure, it's only that we're talking business. It's a matter of wages. The woman folk always approve of them."

Schmidt rolled his eyes heavenward in despair.

"But, when we tell them of the ten per cent. cut! *Ach, Himmel!*"

Cicily turned a startled glance on her husband.

"A ten per cent. cut!" she exclaimed, involuntarily. "Why, Charles!"

Hamilton was annoyed by this unexpected irruption of the feminine into the most serious of business discussions—the intrusion of the female on the financial. He spoke with distinct note of disapproval in his voice:

"Now, Cicily, you know nothing of this."

Delancy, too, added the weight of his accustomed authority.

"Don't bother with things that do not concern you, Cicily." There was a patronizing quality in the admonition that irritated the wife.

Ferguson spoke to the same effect, but with a radically different motive underlying his words:

"Of course, it don't concern you, Mrs. Hamilton. I guess you'll be glad to have some more money to put in bath-tubs and libraries and gymnasiums. No, ma'am, it don't concern you. But it'll make some difference to our wives and daughters, I'm thinking—ten per cent. out of the pay-envelope every week. It'll take the curl out of my Sadie's false hair, all right."

"There will be always some good in everything," Schmidt murmured cynically, but not loud enough for the Yankee to hear.

Cicily was aware of the tension about her, and deemed it the part of wisdom to create a diversion.

"What a coincidence!" she exclaimed, gayly. "Mrs. Schmidt and Mrs. Ferguson and Mrs. McMahon are all coming around here this afternoon. I invited them to attend a meeting of our club."

The dignified face of Mr. Delancy, which was that of the old-school business man, clean-shaven save for the white tufts of side-whisker, was distorted by an emotion of genuine horror; his pink cheeks grew scarlet.

"Cicily!" he gasped.

Hamilton, too, was hardly less disconcerted, for all his familiarity with his wife's equalization whimsies.

"Invited them here?" he questioned, frowning.

The manner of both utterances was of a sort that must inevitably offend the husbands of the women. Cicily, with the sensitiveness of her sex, sought to cover the impression by speaking with a manner of increased enthusiasm.

"Oh, yes," she answered. "Isn't it good of them? They have promised to return my call this afternoon."

Ferguson yielded to a Yankee propensity for dry humour:

"I only hope that Mr. Delancy and Mr. Hamilton won't be too nice to them."

McMahon, too, would have made some comment; but Hamilton, who now perceived his blunder, which might have a disastrous effect on the attitude of these men toward him, hastened to make a diversion on his own account.

"Now, men," he said, as affably as he could contrive, "I've made you acquainted with the difficulties and the necessities of the situation. As I said before, I depend on your loyalty.... Will you let me hear from you later in the afternoon to-day?"

"You'll hear from us, all right," the Yankee assured his employer, with significant emphasis, before Schmidt had a chance to speak; and McMahon nodded agreement.

Once again, Cicily strove to lighten the mood of the men.

"If you're going away to think something over, be sure you come back in time to take your wives home, after they've joined the club. It's the Civitas Society, you know, for the up-lift of women."

No sooner were the members of the committee out of the room than Cicily turned anxiously to her husband.

"Oh, Charles," she exclaimed, "tell me! It's not true, is it, that there's to be a cut in wages at the factory?"

Hamilton turned away impatiently from the appealing face.

"Cicily," he said shortly, "Uncle Jim and I are very busy. We have business of the highest importance to discuss."

Delancy, who from long experience knew much concerning his niece's wilfulness, now read aright the resolute expression on her face. He tugged nervously at his tufts of whisker, and spoke in a tone of resignation:

"Oh, tell her, Charles, and have done with it.... Or, listen, Cicily. It's this way: These men are getting more money than they ought to get. Charles can't make a penny profit, running his business this way. That's all there is to it— he's got to cut them ten per cent. I've advised it, myself."

Cicily's charming nose was now distinctly tip-tilted, whatever might be its normal line.

"Yes, I'd expect you to advise it, Uncle Jim," she remarked, dryly. She turned to her husband, accusingly. "But, Charles, there is no reason why you should follow his advice. Why didn't you ask me? I'm your partner. I don't think you have treated me fairly in this."

Hamilton, overwrought and exasperated by the multiplication of his worries, began a sharp answer; but it was interrupted by the decisiveness with which his wife went on speaking:

"Charles, you have treated me like a child, like a fool.... And you said that you'd let me help you!"

This reproach appealed to Hamilton as grossly unfair.

"Why, Cicily," he exclaimed, "I did let you help. I've let you do everything that you wanted to do—no matter how—" In a sudden access of discretion, he choked back the "foolish."

Delancy, presuming on the right of criticism that had been his during the years of guardianship, spoke with a candor that was not flattering.

"He let you do more than I'd have let you do. He let you waste your money on bath-tubs and libraries, and such foolishness, to make the men dissatisfied. I wish somebody would tell me what a man working for two dollars a day can do with a bath-tub and a library at the works."

"If anybody were to tell you, you wouldn't listen," was Cicily's pert retort.

Delancy tugged at his wisp of whisker, and wagged his head dolefully.

"I don't know what young women these days are coming to," was his melancholy comment.

"What you men are driving us to, you mean!" Cicily fairly snapped. It was difficult enough to manage her husband, without having her position jeopardized by the interference of this meddlesome old man, who stood for that exclusion of her sex against which she was fighting. She went to the chair in which Ferguson had been sitting, and reclined there in a posture of graceful ease that was far from expressing the turmoil of her spirit. As he watched her movements, and studied the loveliness of her, with her delicate face aglow and her amber eyes brilliant in this mood of excitement, Hamilton forgot his worriment for the moment in uxorious admiration. He was smiling fondly on his wife, even as Delancy uttered an exclamation of rebuke to him:

"And you're her husband!" His emphasis made it clear that a husband like himself would have suppressed such insubordination long ago.

"Well," Hamilton replied placidly, and with a hint of amusement in his voice, "you brought her up, you know."

"I did not—no such thing!" the old man spluttered. In his indignation, he pulled so viciously on a whisker that he winced from the pain, which by no means tended to soothe his ruffled temper.

"You're quite right, Uncle Jim," Cicily agreed, with dangerous sweetness in the musical voice. "Of course, you never had any time to pay attention to me, or to Aunt Emma either, for that matter. Oh, no, you were too much absorbed in that horrid business of yours. You drove Aunt Emma into working for the heathen, and incidentally, you did teach me one thing: you taught me what sort of a wife not to be. I learned from you never to be married after the fashion in which you and Aunt Emma are married."

Delancy was not blest with an overabundant sense of humor. Now, he forgot the general charge against him in shocked surprise over the final statement, which he took literally.

"Look here, Cicily," he remonstrated. "It took twenty-two minutes in the old First Presbyterian Church to marry your Aunt Emma and me. You couldn't possibly get a more binding ceremony."

Cicily laughed disdainfully.

"Well, it's my opinion that you've never been married at all, really," she persisted, with a bantering seriousness. "You wouldn't have been really married if you had spent two whole days in the church." Then, in answer to the pained amazement expressed on her uncle's face, she continued succinctly: "Yes, I mean it, Uncle Jim. Aunt Emma has been second wife ever since those twenty-two minutes in the old First Presbyterian Church, to which you referred so feelingly.... And she has my sympathy. You married business first, and Aunt Emma afterward. Business had the first claim, and has always kept first place. That's why Aunt Emma has my sympathy."

Delancy rose from his chair, greatly offended, now that he perceived the manner in which he had been bamboozled by the wayward humor of his niece. He moved toward the door at a pace as hurried as dignity would permit. There, he turned to address his disrespectful former ward.

"Charles has my sympathy!" he growled; and stalked from the room.

"Don't forget that you are coming to dinner on Sunday—with your second wife!" the irrepressible Cicily called after him impertinently. But, if the reminder was heard, it was not answered; and husband and wife were left alone together.

Hamilton would have remonstrated with his bride over her wholly unnecessary irritating of her uncle, but he was not given an opportunity. Before the door was fairly shut behind her offended relation, Cicily took the war into the enemy's camp by a curt question:

"Now, Charles, why do you cut wages?"

"Because I have to," was the prompt response.

"And why didn't you tell me?"

"Tell you? Nonsense!" The man's tone was expressive of extreme annoyance.

"But I'm your partner," Cicily persisted bravely, although her heart sank under the rebuff. "You yourself said that I was."

"Well, and so you are, since you want it so," Hamilton admitted; "and you're attending to your end, aren't you?"

"Yes, the little end," Cicily agreed, disparagingly.

At that, Hamilton was plainly exasperated.

"What end did you expect?" he demanded. "I tell you, Cicily," he continued, in the tone of one arguing with labored patience to convince a child of some truism, "that business is too big, too serious, too strong for a woman like you, my dear."

"Yes, that's just the fear that grips my heart sometimes, Charles," the wife admitted. With an ingenuity characteristic of her active intelligence, she had perceived a method whereby to twist his words to her own purpose. "Look here!" she went on in a caressing voice, utterly unlike the emphatic one in which she had spoken hitherto. "Do you for a moment imagine that I really like business? Well, then, I don't—not a little bit! For that matter, hardly any woman does, I fancy. As to myself, Charles, I'm afraid of it—that's the whole truth. I'm only in it to watch it—and you!"

The change in her manner had immediate effect on the husband. Again, he was surveying her with eyes in which admiration shone. For the ten-thousandth time, he was reveling in the beauty of that oval contour, in the tender curves of the scarlet lips.... But he forgot to voice his thoughts. Indeed, what need? He had told her so many times already!

"You talk as if business were a woman," he said, with a smile of conscious sex superiority, "and as if you were jealous."

Cicily concealed her resentment of the patronizing manner, and replied with no apparent diminution in her amiability:

"That's just it: I am jealous!"

"Good heavens!" Hamilton cried, indignantly. "Surely, you know that I never think twice of any woman I meet in business."

The wife smiled in high disdain.

"Woman!" she ejaculated, with scornful emphasis. "I'm not in the least afraid of any woman being more to you than I am, Charles. Just let one try!"

"Why, what would you do?" Hamilton inquired, curiously.

The answer was swift and vigorous, pregnant with the insolent consciousness of power that is the prerogative of a lovely woman. Cicily leaned forward in her chair, and the golden eyes darkened and flashed.

"Why, I'd beat her! I'd be everything to you that she was—and more. I'd outdress her, I'd out-talk her, I'd outwit her, I'd out-think her. I'd play on your love and on your masculine jealousy. Oh, there'd be plenty of men to play the play with me. I'd be more alluring, more fascinating, more difficult, until I held you safe again in the hollow of my hand, and then—why, then, I'd be very much tempted to throw you away!"

The verve with which this girl-woman thus vaunted her skill in the use of those charms that dominate the opposite sex thrilled and fascinated the lover, pierced the reserve that possession had overcast on ardor. His cheeks flushed, under the provocation of the glances with which she marked the allurements of which she was the mistress. As she finished speaking, he sprang up from his chair, caught her in his arms, and drew her passionately to his breast. But Cicily avoided the kiss he would have pressed on her lips. With her mouth at his ear, she whispered, plaintively now, no longer boastful, only a timid, fearing, jealous woman:

"Yes, I can fight a rival who is a woman, Charles, and I can win. But this other rival, this fascinating monstrous, evil goddess—ah!"

Hamilton held his wife away from him by the shoulders, mid regarded her in bewilderment.

"Evil goddess!" he repeated, half in doubt as to her meaning.

"Surely, she must be that," Cicily declared, firmly; "this spirit who is the goddess of modern business, whom I feel absorbing you day by day, taking from me more and ever more of your thoughts, of your heart, of your soul, changing you in every vital way, and doing it in spite of all that I can do, though I fight against her with all my strength! Oh, it's terrible, the hopelessness of it all! Some day all of you will be gone, forever!"

"Swallowed up by the evil spirit?" Hamilton asked, quizzically, with a smile.

"Yes!" The answer was given with a seriousness that rebuked his levity in the presence of possible catastrophe.

The husband repeated his threadbare argument.

"But, dear," he urged gently, "you know that I love you just the same."

There was a curious, cynical sadness in the wife's voice as she replied:

"Probably, a man under ether loves one just the same. But who wants to be loved by a man under ether?"

"Cicily, you exaggerate!" Hamilton exclaimed. He dropped his hands from her shoulders, and reseated himself, while she remained standing before him. There was petulance in his inflection when he spoke again: "I have you, and I have my business."

Cicily made a *moué* that sufficiently expressed her weariness of this time-worn fact.

"Your two loves!" she said, bitterly. "Now, at this moment, you think that they're equal. Well, perhaps they are—at this moment. Some day, the crisis will come. Then, you'll have to choose. It's a new triangle, Charles—the twentieth-century triangle in America: the wife, the husband and the business. But remember: when the choice comes for us, I shall not be an Aunt Emma!"

The manner of his wife, as well as her words, disturbed the husband strangely. Never had she seemed more appealing in her loveliness, never more daintily alluring to the eye of a man; yet, never had she seemed to hold herself so coldly aloof, to be so impersonally remote. He felt a longing to draw her again into the gentle trustfulness of the maiden who had gloried in his love.

"What do you want me to do, dear?" he questioned. "I told you that you could help me. I let you help."

Cicily seated herself again before she replied. When, at last, she spoke, her voice was listless:

"Yes; you let me spend some of my own money for luxuries. It seems that I could have used it to better advantage in helping to pay the men their wages, and thus save you from a possible strike."

"No," was the serious response. "At best, that would have been only a makeshift—putting off the evil day. No; this thing must be fought out, once for all. We are running at a loss. To take money from you would be merely to waste it. Let me tell you, too, that there isn't a chance in the world for the Hamilton factory in the event of a strike."

Cicily seized on the admission as favoring her side of the argument.

"Then, you must not cut the wages," she declared, with spirit. "You must fight Morton and Carrington."

"How can one man fight the trust?" Hamilton questioned, in return. "No, I'm caught between the two millstones: Morton, Carrington, the trust, above; the men, labor, below. To live, I must cut into the men. That's business."

"Now, I know it isn't right," Cicily exclaimed. "Tell me," she continued, bending forward in her eagerness, until he could watch the beating pulse of her round throat, "if I were to give you all my money, couldn't you fight, and yet keep up the wages? I have quite a lot, you know. It was accumulating, uncle said, all the time while I was growing up." She refused to be convinced by her husband's shake of the head in negation. "I've met a lot of their women and children, in these last few weeks, while I have been—playing at being in business. None of the families have any more than enough for their needs—I know! Some of them have barely that. A cut in wages will be something awful in its effects. Why, Charles, some of the families have six or seven children."

"I know," the harassed employer acknowledged, with a sigh that was almost a groan. "But, Cicily, my dear, unless there is a cut, I shall be ruined. That is the long and the short of the matter. Unless I make the men suffer a little now, the factory must be closed down; all Dad's work must go for nothing. It's either I or them. If they don't take the cut for the time being, they'll soon be without any wages at all. Now, if you really want to help me, in a way to count, just do all you possibly can to prevent a strike. Then, you'll be helping me, and, too, you'll be helping them as well. Of course, you understand that I shall put back the wages as soon as ever I can."

"Good!" the wife cried, happily. "I'll help." Despite her distress over the situation as it affected both the workmen and her husband, she was elated by the fact that, at last, she was wholly within her husband's confidence; that, at last, she was actually to coöperate with him in his business concerns: a practical, no longer merely a theoretical, partner! Hamilton himself gave the cap to the climax of her delight.

"Now," he said, with a tender smile, "you're positively in business, according to your heart's desire. You're on the inside, all ready to fight the what-do-you-call-it."

But a new thought had changed the mood of the impulsive bride. Of a sudden, she sobered, and her eyes widened in fear.

"Yes," she said slowly, tremulously; "I'll help you, Charles, in any way that I can, for a strike would be too terrible. It would come between you and me."

Small wonder that, Hamilton was astounded by this declaration on the part of his wife. His usually firm jaw relaxed, dropped; he sat staring at the fair woman opposite him with unrestrained amazement.

"How under heaven could a strike at the factory come between you and me?" he queried, at last.

The answer was slow in coming; but it came, none the less—came firmly, unhesitatingly, unequivocally.

"If there were to be a strike, I could not let those women and those children suffer without doing something to help them."

At this candid statement as to what her course would be, the husband stiffened in his chair. His expression grew severe, minatory.

"What?" he ejaculated, harshly. "You'd use your money to help them? My wife use her money to fight me?" His frown was savage.

Cicily preserved her appearance of calm confidence, although she was woefully minded to cower back, and to cover her eyes from the menace in his. She was a woman of strongly fixed principles, however chimerical her ideas in some directions, and now her conscience drove her on, when love would have bade her retreat.

"I'd use my money to keep women and children from starving to death," she said, in a low voice, which trembled despite her will.

Hamilton smothered an angry imprecation. He strove to master his wrath as he spoke again, very sternly:

"Cicily, you are my wife. You have said that you were my partner. As either, as both, you have responsibilities toward my welfare that must be respected."

"I'm a woman, with responsibilities as a human being first of all," was the undaunted retort. "I wouldn't be fit to be a wife, if I were to let women and children starve without trying to help."

"Nonsense, Cicily!" Hamilton's anger was controlled now; but he remained greatly incensed over this stubborn folly on his wife's part, as he esteemed it. "Strikers don't starve to death, nowadays. They have benefits and funds, and all sorts of things, to help them. They don't even go hungry."

"Then, why do they ever give in?" was the pertinent query. "I tell you they do go hungry—often, even at the best of times. I've been down among those people. I've seen them with three, six, children to feed and clothe, and rent to pay, on two to four dollars a day. What chance have they to save? I tell you, if there's a strike, some of them will starve, and, if you let them starve, Charles, you won't be my husband!"

"Cicily!"

"I mean it." The wife rose from her chair, went to her husband, and kissed him, tenderly, sorrowfully. Then, she turned to leave the room.

But, before she reached the door, Hamilton spoke again, gravely, quite without anger:

"Cicily, my dear," he said, "I give you credit for being as sincere and honest as you are foolish. So, the only chance for all of us is that you should do your best now, at once, to prevent an issue that may spell catastrophe for all of us. It's up to you now, my dear partner, to do your best to win them, to keep them from striking."

The young wife paused in the doorway, and faced her husband. There was a trace of tears veiling the radiance of the golden eyes. Her voice quivered, but the low music of it was very earnest:

"I will, Charles—I will fight hard—my hardest—for my happiness and for yours!"

CHAPTER IX

Mrs. Schmidt, Mrs. McMahon and Miss Sadie Ferguson, whom Cicily had selected as the principal beneficiaries in her initial work of up-lift, arrived a half-hour before the time set for the meeting of the Civitas Society, and were shown into the drawing-room. Mrs. Schmidt, a thin wisp of faded womanhood, effaced herself in a remote corner, while Mrs. McMahon, a brawny Amazon with red, round face and shrewdly twinkling eyes, frankly wandered about the room, scrutinizing the furnishings and ornaments and commenting on them without restraint. Sadie Ferguson, on the other hand, seated herself elegantly upright on an upholstered chair, and disported herself altogether after the manner of heroines of high degree as described by her favorite Brooklyn author. At times, she stared intently, as some impressive thing strange to her experience caught her eye; but always she recalled her manners speedily, and forthwith relapsed into a languid indifference of demeanor such as becomes the Vere De Vere. The trio had not long to wait before their hostess appeared, and greeted them with a genuine cordiality that put them at their ease, as far as ease was possible in an environment so novel. She was at pains to pay a compliment to the girl:

"Prettier than ever, Sadie!" she exclaimed, with honest admiration. And, in fact, the girl would have been charming, but for the disfiguring effects of an over-gaudy dress and an abominable hat.

"Aw, quit yer kiddin'," Sadie answered coquettishly, intensely pleased and quite forgetting the Vere De Vere manner in her pleasure over the compliment. An expression of horror came in her face, as she realized her violent departure from the ideal; and she added stammeringly: "I mean, you're really too kind, my dear Mrs. Hamilton." Having achieved this, the girl drew a long breath of relief. She felt that she had redeemed herself in the matter of social elegance.

Cicily smiled pleasantly on Sadie, then turned to Mrs. McMahon, for she was minded to put these women in the best of humors, in order thus to work toward the avoidance of a strike by means of their influence over their husbands. She observed the hat that had been the cause of McMahon's complaint, which was, in truth, a riot of variegated ugliness. Cicily believed, however, that in this instance the end must justify the means.

"What a beautiful hat!" she cried, in a tone of convincing sincerity. She even clasped her hands to emphasize her admiration.

Mrs. McMahon preened herself, and tossed her head; so that feathers and flowers dashed their hues worse than before.

"It's nothing so much! It's just some odds and ends they threw together for me!"

"Odds and ends!" Cicily repeated, in a hushed voice; and she added, truthfully: "I never saw anything like it in my life." She purposely avoided directly addressing Mrs. Schmidt, for she was aware of the woman's painful shyness. "It was ever so good of you to come around this afternoon," she went on. "I'm going to have some friends here to meet you."

"Gentleman friends?" Sadie questioned, eagerly. Her face fell when Cicily answered in the negative, and she could not restrain an ejaculation of disappointment.

Mrs. McMahon felt it incumbent on her to administer a rebuke to the girl.

"What do you care, Sadie, so long as they're Mrs. Hamilton's friends?" And she added majestically, turning to her hostess: "Excuse her, ma'am."

At this public correction, Sadie flushed scarlet, and glanced appealingly toward Mrs. Schmidt.

"What a nerve!" she commented, angrily. Then, she addressed Mrs. McMahon herself. "If you will pardon me, Mrs. McMahon," she said, very haughtily, "I prefer to present my own apologies in individual person." And, finally, she turned to Cicily. "Mrs. Hamilton, if you consider my interrogation regarding the sex of your guests impertinent, my humblest apologies are at your disposal."

"And she didn't choke!" the Irishwoman murmured, admiringly.

Cicily insisted that there was no occasion for apology, and afterward went on to explain something as to the character and aims of the Civitas Society for the Uplift of Women. But here, at once, she found herself beset with unexpected difficulties. Mrs. McMahon drew herself up with all the dignity of her great bulk, and voiced her feeling by the tone in which she asked:

"I would like to know, Mrs. Hamilton, if you think we are subjects for uplifting?"

"Can you beat it!" Sadie cried, in outraged pride.

Cicily hastened to soothe her guests by an explanation that was more ingenious than ingenuous.

"You don't understand," she remonstrated. "This is the club I spoke to you about. I want you to become members of the society. We need you to help in the work."

"You're on!" Sadie declared, with gusto. Again, she realized how she had departed from her idols. "I would say," she went on mincingly, "it will afford me great pleasure."

"You mean, then," Mrs. McMahon inquired, "that you've picked us out to help uplift the other women?" As Cicily nodded assent, she continued, condescendingly: "Well, if I do have to say it myself, there's many of them as needs it."

Presently, Mrs. Carrington and Mrs. Morton were shown into the drawing-room, and welcomed by Cicily, who insisted on introducing them to "three other earnest workers." The newcomers submitted to the introductions with obvious unwillingness, and their acknowledgments were of the frigidest.

"They," Cicily explained, with a wave of her hand toward the three, "have had large practical experience in the work of the club."

"Sure, and I have that," Mrs. McMahon agreed, expansively; "and so have Frieda and Sadie—in a smaller way, of course."

Mrs. Carrington unbent so far as to ejaculate, "Indeed!" the while she surveyed the speaker through a lorgnette; and Mrs. Morton added an unenthusiastic, "Really!"

Cicily, who was all anxiety to establish harmonious relations between the two parties of her guests, since so much might depend on the result of her efforts, spoke placatingly to the company:

"I'm sure you ladies will find one another entertaining."

"Oh, vastly entertaining, no doubt!" Mrs. Morton replied; but her tone was far from satisfactory to the worried hostess. Nor was the manner of Mrs. McMahon calculated to relieve the tension.

"If I live, I'll have the time of my life!" she declared, grimly. She turned to Mrs. Morton: "Is your husband's family any relation to the Mortons of County Clare, if I may make so bold as to ask?"

"Yes," Mrs. Morton answered, with much complacency. "Mr. Morton at present keeps up his old family estate in Ireland."

"Sure, and that wouldn't bust him," Mrs. McMahon commented caustically. "I remember the estate—a bit of a cabin in a bog." The Amazon's huge frame shook as she chuckled. "Just ask your husband; he'll remember me well. Sure, the last time I saw him was when his aunt, Nora, married Tom McMahon, my husband's uncle. Faith, it's cousins we are by marriage."

What might have been Mrs. Morton's attitude toward this suddenly discovered kinship must remain forever in doubt; for, to Cicily's unbounded relief, a diversion was now offered by the appearance on the scene of Mrs. Flynn, Miss Johnson and Ruth Howard. Once again, the necessary introductions were made. Mrs. Flynn displayed astonishment at the style of these "ladies," but contrived a neutral manner that was void of offense. Miss Johnson was distant, but Ruth was honestly pleased with this opportunity for sisterly association for the sake of uplift, and rolled her large eyes ecstatically.

"These ladies," Cicily explained anew, "are the members whom the club has met to consider. They have had wide experience in the great work of helping women."

"Indeed, and you're right, Mrs. Hamilton," Mrs. McMahon affirmed. "Whenever anything happens on the block, it's Katy McMahon they send for. Faith, setting-ups and laying-outs are my specialties."

Mrs. Carrington and Mrs. Morton had withdrawn to a *tête-à-tête* at some distance, where they were engaged in a low-toned conversation, punctuated by many head-shakings. The hostess had seated the new arrivals in chairs opposite Mrs. McMahon and Sadie. It was evident by their exclamations that Mrs. Flynn and Ruth were mystified and impressed by the Irishwoman's explanation. But Miss Johnson maintained an air of impenetrable reserve.

"Setting-ups!" quoth the militant suffragette.

"Laying-outs!" sighed Ruth; and she turned up her eyes, with a blink of inquiry.

"Yes," Mrs. McMahon went on, unctuously; "setting up with the sick, and laying out the dead. Faith, sometimes, I have to be nurse and undertaker, all in one."

"So," Ruth gushed, unrolling her eyes with some difficulty, "sitting up with the sick, and laying out the dead, is your great work!"

"Oh, not that entirely," the Irishwoman continued, "not that entirely! Of course, I have to run my house; and, now and then, when a family's too poor to have a doctor, 'tis myself that brings a baby into the world on the side, so to speak. Having had five myself, I'm quite familiar with the how of it."

There came a horrified gasp from the women listening.

"Cheese it!" Sadie whispered, fiercely. From her study of the favorite author, she surmised that Mrs. McMahon was wandering far afield from the small talk of a Clara Vere De Vere. "Your subject for conversation is really positively shocking and disgusting," she added, aloud.

Cicily attempted yet once again to establish harmony among discordant elements.

"Mrs. McMahon has done so much good in homes of suffering," she said gently, "that she's very direct in her speech."

The good-natured Irishwoman herself chose to make the *amende honorable*, but after her own fashion.

"Sure, excuse me, ladies," she exclaimed, heartily. "Faith, I didn't mean to speak of anything so unfashionable as the bearing of children."

Mrs. Delancy and a friend entered at this moment, to the great relief of Cicily, who greeted her kinswoman warmly, and at once led her toward Mrs. McMahon.

"Here is someone whom you know, Aunt Emma," she said, with significant emphasis.

Mrs. Delancy, after one look of shocked amazement at the unwieldy figure squeezed into a gilt chair, which threatened momentarily to collapse under the unaccustomed burden, recovered the poise of the well-bred woman of unquestioned social position, and went forward cordially, holding out her hand.

"Oh, it's Mrs. McMahon!" she exclaimed, with a pleasant smile. "I'm delighted to have you with us in this work."

Under this geniality, all of the Irishwoman's resentment vanished, and she returned the greeting warmly.

"And how is little Jimmy?" Mrs. Delancy continued, returning to Mrs. McMahon, after having spoken to Mrs. Schmidt and Sadie.

Thus addressed, the maternal Amazon displayed certain evidences of confusion, and, indeed, seemed inclined to evade the issue, for she replied after a little hesitation:

"Sure, ma'am, Michael and Terence and Patrick and Katy and Nora are all fine."

"And Jimmy?" Mrs. Delancy persisted, albeit somewhat puzzled by the woman's manner.

"Well, ma'am," Mrs. McMahon made answer, with an embarrassment that was a stranger to her "you see, ma'am, there's only five, at present.... We haven't had Jimmy yet!"

There came a gasping chorus from the whole company. Cicily, who had taken her position behind the table set for the presiding officer of the Civitas Club, lifted a scarlet face, as she beat a tattoo with the gavel, and called out bravely:

"The Civitas Society will now come to order!"

CHAPTER X

There was a little delay while the members of the club shifted positions in such manner as to bring them facing the president. When this had been accomplished, the militant suffragette at once stood up, and spoke with the aggressive energy that marked her every act.

"I move that we dispense with the reading of the minutes of the last meeting."

"Yes, I think we ought to," Cicily agreed, and she smiled approval on Mrs. Flynn. "In fact, there were no minutes."

But Mrs. Carrington nourished rancor against her rival for the presidency, and the fact that Mrs. Flynn had made a suggestion, was reason enough why she should combat it.

"I think," she remarked coldly, getting to her feet slowly, "that we should certainly read the minutes. It's most interesting to read the minutes." She re-seated herself, with an air of great importance.

"But," Cicily objected, "there are no minutes."

Mrs. Carrington did not trouble to rise for her retort:

"I don't see what that has to do with the question at issue."

"Oh, very well, then," Cicily rejoined, with one of those flashes of inspiration that were of such service to her as a presiding officer, "you read them yourself, Mrs. Carrington." At this happy suggestion, Mrs. Carrington uttered an ejaculation, but vouchsafed nothing more precise. Cicily waited for a few seconds, then continued gaily: "Now that the minutes are read, the specific business before the house is the consideration of new members. All working clubs to be successful must take in constantly virile, live members."

Mrs. Morton, who had by no means forgotten her conversation with Mrs. McMahon and cherished a distinct grudge against that excellent woman, voiced a caution:

"But, Mrs. Hamilton," she objected, "due care should be exercised in the selection."

"The club cannot be too careful," Mrs. Carrington agreed.

Mrs. McMahon was fuming in her chair, evidently on the edge of an outbreak. Mrs. Delancy saved the situation by prompt action.

"I think," she said, rising, "that, if new members are to be voted on, they should not be present in the meeting during the discussion."

"Oh, yes," Cicily made decision, with a smile of gratitude for her aunt. She nodded brightly toward the three candidates, and addressed them in her most winning voice.

"Mrs. McMahon, will you and Mrs. Schmidt and Miss Ferguson kindly await the club's action in the next room?" She indicated the curtained archway that led into the withdrawing-room at the back.

"Certainly, ma'am," the Irishwoman answered, with a rough haughtiness all her own. She heaved herself up from the gilt chair, which seemed to creak a sigh of relief; and the trio went out in the midst of a deep silence.

Their departure set free a babel of chatter, a great part of it addressed in personal remonstrance to the presiding officer. Cicily lost patience, and called out sharply, with the authority of her office:

"Any member addressing the chair will please follow the usual parliamentary procedure!"

Mrs. Carrington was the first to take advantage of the formal method. Sitting elegantly in her place, she spoke:

"Madam Chairman, I rise to a point of order."

"Very well, then, Mrs. Carrington," Cicily rejoined, with her most official manner, "please rise."

The outraged member bounced to her feet with an alacrity that was not her habit. It was evident that the lady was angry.

"Really," she declared in an acid voice, "I never in my whole life—"

"What was your point of order?" Cicily interrupted, blandly.

"Why, well—well—that is, I've forgotten it now. But it was very big!"

The presiding officer's sense of humor ran away with her discretion.

"The chair," she announced gravely, "regrets exceedingly that the member found her point of order too big to raise."

It was Mrs. Delancy who, after her usual fashion, strove to restore peace, as Mrs. Carrington indignantly settled back into her chair:

"Madam Chairman, if this meeting is called to consider the election of new members, I would like to nominate Mrs. McMahon, Mrs. Schmidt and Miss Ferguson."

Ruth now made display of her customary need for information. She turned her large eyes on the presiding officer, and inquired plaintively:

"How do you elect new members?"

Cicily explained with an air of patient toleration.

"They must first be nominated, my dear, and then be seconded. You have a chance of performing a valuable service to the club now, Ruth, by seconding the nominations already made."

"Oh, have I?" the girl demanded, animatedly, evidently pleased by this unexpected opportunity of fulfilling her ideals. "Well, then, I second them—yes, every one of them!"

"It is moved and seconded," Cicily stated briskly, "that Mrs. McMahon, Mrs. Schmidt and Miss Sadie Ferguson be elected as members of the Civitas Society for the Uplift of Women and the Spread of Social Equality among the Masses."

The militant suffragette was on her feet before the presiding officer had finished speaking.

"Madam Chairman," she announced in her resonant voice, "I rise on a question of rules."

"But there is a question before the house," Cicily protested.

"I am exceedingly sorry to antagonize the chair," Mrs. Flynn maintained resolutely, "but, since my late lamentable experience in this club, I have made it a point to look up the matter of parliamentary law as exercised in America." By way of verification, she held aloft a formidable-appearing, fat volume. "Now, I would like to know whether members are elected to this club by a plurality of votes, or by a two-thirds majority, or whether or no a single adverse vote can keep out a candidate from the privileges of the club."

"A plurality is quite sufficient, Mrs. Flynn, I assure you," Cicily decided without the slightest hesitation, despite the fact that her knowledge as to the difference, if any, between plurality and majority was of the vaguest. "Now, all in favor of the candidates, please—"

Once again, her purpose was frustrated by the suffragette, who had been busily consulting the formidable volume.

"A moment, Madam Chairman," she demanded, peremptorily. "This American book on parliamentary law says that the club has the right to decide how new members are to be elected. Therefore, I move that these elections be as the elections in England, made by secret voting, and that three black balls be sufficient to defeat any candidate in her candidacy."

"I second the motion," Miss Johnson called out, rallying to the support of Mrs. Flynn as on a former occasion, because she believed that such action would tend toward the annoyance of her dear friends, Mrs. Carrington and Cicily.

Cicily forthwith offered the motion to a vote, and it was carried, although Mrs. Carrington, Mrs. Morton and Mrs. Delancy voted against it.

Immediately, Mrs. Flynn brought to view from a mysterious pocket a small black box of wood.

"I have here," she explained impressively, "the voting-box used in our club in England. I'm very sorry we did not have it on the occasion of the election of the president at the last session of this club. I have no doubt that the issue would have been quite otherwise. Yet, I hope that no one will misunderstand my position. It is merely my tendency toward the strong upholding of constitutional rights as opposed unalterably and forever to tyranny and the forces of disorder and anarchy. Naturally, there can be no doubt as to the ultimate election of one at least of the candidates in this particular instance, inasmuch as that particular candidate is the relation of a member of the Civitas Society."

Mrs. Morton flounced out of her seat, with an agility that showed her full appreciation of the thrust.

"It is unconstitutional for one club-member to insult a fellow club-member," she cried, in a rage. "And, anyhow, I wish to deny that statement. I'm not a relation—I'm not, I'm not!"

"Pardon me," the militant suffragette declared, belligerently. Her narrow, sallow face was set; the lust of battle shone in her snapping eyes. "I know that in Ireland the Mortons and the McMahons are close relatives. Being an Englishwoman, I naturally know all about it."

Cicily deemed this a fitting time for the exercise of her prerogative as presiding officer, and rapped violently on the table with the gavel.

"Order! Order!" she commanded. Then, she beamed approvingly on Mrs. Flynn.

"Will you carry the box around, Mrs. Flynn, please?" she requested.

The suffragette courteously acquiesced, and, as a formal return to the chair for the honor bestowed on her, first presented the box to Cicily, who under instructions as to the manner of operation dropped a white ball into the receptacle, after exhibiting it ostentatiously so that all the company could see. Next, Mrs. Flynn offered the box to Mrs. Morton, who selected a black ball, and permitted all who would to observe the color before her vote was concealed within the box.

"I congratulate you on your triumph over natural family affection," the presiding officer remarked, bitterly.

In turn, the box was presented to each of the members present. This task accomplished, Mrs. Flynn, at the request of Cicily, set herself to counting the votes, while the idle ladies discussed the exciting events of the session with great animation. Presently, the teller looked up, and addressed the chair.

"Madam Chairman," she announced in a businesslike tone, "the vote stands eight to two."

At this statement, the presiding officer clapped her hands merrily, in a manner more joyous than dignified.

"Good!" she cried, and her dainty smile was all-embracing, as her happy eyes roved over the assembly. "Then, they're all elected, after all. It's great! Oh, I thank you! I knew our club would vindicate itself. I knew that you would live up to our motto—whatever it is. I knew that you were too big to let social prejudices stand in the way of the progress of real womanhood. I knew that we were actually a live club, come together with a genuine aim to do real good. I can see now that we are going to accomplish something worth while. We are not going to be merely a set of empty-headed, silly women with nothing to do. Oh, I tell you that I have some great plans, now that at last we are really started out right. Now, we can outline our plans of work among women less fortunate than we ourselves. We can find places for them, we can lead them on to better things, we can teach them our own doctrine of living for others, our own principle of making other people happy." The young wife had spoken with an ever increasing enthusiasm. Her eyes were sparkling; her voice deepened musically; the color glowed brightly in her cheeks; her slender form was held proudly erect in the tense eagerness of an exalted sincerity of purpose. The other women listened wonderingly at first; but, little by little, the eloquent vehemence of their president moved them to sympathetic excitement, so that they nodded and smiled assent to the speaker's lofty sentiments.

Only Mrs. Flynn seemed entirely unaffected by the oratorical outburst. Now, when the speech came to a close, that militant suffragette again addressed the chair.

"Madam Chairman," she said with brutal directness, "the vote stands eight to two. There are two white balls, and eight black balls."

At this shocking revelation of the fact, Cicily stared dazedly for a moment; then, an expression of bleak disappointment stole over her features. She uttered a sound of dismay, which was almost a moan, and the color fled from her face.

"Oh, I don't—can't believe it!" she cried, with sudden fierceness. With the words, she snatched up the box, which Mrs. Flynn had deposited on the table, and poured out the balls. She stared at them affrightedly for a moment. There could be no mistake: They were two white and eight black! Cicily regarded the incontrovertible evidence of defeat for a minute with dilated eyes. Then, abruptly, she laughed hardily, straightened up from her scrutiny of the balls, and gazed wrathfully out upon her fellow club-members. When she spoke, her tone was of ice. Her utterance was made with the utmost of deliberation.

"So," she said, while her amber eyes flashed fire, "you are a set of empty-headed, silly women with nothing to do, after all!"

"Cicily!" Mrs. Delancy exclaimed, aghast, while the others could only gasp in horror before this unparalleled vituperation.

"I mean it—every word of it!" Cicily repeated, hotly. But the impetuosity of her mood was checked as she beheld the general consternation consequent on her attack; for now all the others were on their feet, moving hurriedly and muttering excitedly.

"I suppose this is parliamentary law as it is understood in America," the militant suffragette made sarcastic comment, in a shrill voice. "I prefer the English fashion of doing things, for my part."

Cicily realized, with an increase of misery, how intolerable had been her conduct. With that swift changefulness that was distinctive of her nature, she sought to make amends as best she could, although she understood that the task was well-nigh a hopeless one.

"I beg your pardon," she said, with as much humility as she could summon. "But, oh, you don't know what you are doing. You can't know! Don't you realize that you are spoiling our one chance for doing good—spoiling our chance to make this a genuine club to help women actually, not just merely making a joke by pretending?"

Mrs. Morton voiced the general sentiment of disagreement succinctly:

"I fail to see how association with such persons could be anything but distasteful, even disgusting."

"Exactly!" Mrs. Carrington agreed.

"Such women have their own clubs," Miss Johnson pointed out for the enlightenment of the presiding officer. She was very happy over her dear Cicily's discomfiture. "How can they help in any really great work? Let them work among the creatures of their own class. We," she concluded loftily, "have our ideals."

"My ideal," the president retorted bitterly, "is to do something—not merely to talk about it. Not one of you," she continued, waxing wroth again, "has ever done any real good, has ever put herself out to be of service to others, has ever really done anything for anybody else—not one of you!"

"Mrs. Hamilton," Mrs. Morton protested indignantly, "I cannot permit such a statement. I for one send my check to the Charity Organization every Christmas, without fail." Others, too, boasted of their philanthropies, always exercised through some most respectable medium. As the clamor of rebuke died away, Cicily ventured one more plea:

"Then, won't you do this for me?" she asked. "I, as your president, ask that you elect these women. Let them in, to help me in doing the hard work. You needn't do anything, but just belong and take the credit. I am under obligations to these persons. I promised them election to the club. I know now that I had no right to do so, but I did. I am sorry that I was so hasty in the matter. But won't you make my word good in this one case?" The musical voice was tenderly persuasive. Some of those who listened yielded to the spell of it and the winning radiance of the amber eyes. But Mrs. Flynn was not of these.

"There's nothing in this book of American parliamentary law that says the president has a right to promise anything binding on the club. I move that the president consider herself rebuked for exceeding her authority."

"Ruth, there's another chance to second something," Cicily suggested, ironically.

The maiden of the large eyes was pleased and flattered by the suggestion, which she accepted in all seriousness.

"Really?" she exclaimed, and turned her gaze aloft. "Oh, then, I second it— I second it, of course!"

"It is moved and seconded," Cicily declared listlessly, "that the president be rebuked for trying to be of some genuine use to herself and to her fellow women. All in favor of the motion will please say ay."

The form in which the president had stated the motion was not satisfactory to most of the members, who preserved a silence of indecision, with the single exception of Ruth, who uttered an enthusiastic affirmative vote, as a matter of course, only to shrink back perplexedly when she found angry eyes focused on her from every side. But Cicily nonchalantly announced the motion as having been carried, without troubling to call for the contrary vote.

"Ladies," she said, "the president accepts the rebuke; and she also resigns from her office and from the club. She is done with you, with all of you, and with your pitiful joke of a club."

She stood serenely defiant, while the company of babbling, head-tossing women hastened forth from the drawing-room, until only Mrs. Delancy remained.

CHAPTER XI

For a few moments after the passing of the Civitas Society, Cicily remained in her place, motionless, tense, her face whitely set. Then, of a sudden, the rigidity of her pose relaxed. She moved swiftly to where her aunt was sitting, dropped to her knees, and buried her face in the old lady's lap. The dainty form was shaken by a storm of sobs.... Mrs. Delancy, wise from years, attempted no word of comfort for the time being—only stroked the shining brown tresses softly, and patted a shoulder tenderly. So, the girl, for now she was no more than that, wept out the first fury of her grief in this comforting, sheltering presence, as so often she had done in the years before marriage claimed her. Little by little, the fierceness of her emotion was worn out, until at last she was able to raise a sorrow-stricken face, in which the clear gold of the eyes still shone beautiful, though dimmed, through the veil of tears. The scarlet lips were tremulous, and the notes of the musical voice came brokenly as she spoke her despair.

"I've ruined him!" came the hopeless wail.

Mrs. Delancy misunderstood the final pronoun, for the articulation of the girl, clogged by feeling, was none too distinct.

"Pooh!" she ejaculated, cheerfully. "For my part, I think you're well rid of them."

"But you don't understand," Cicily almost moaned. "It's him—him! I've ruined him, I tell you."

This time, Mrs. Delancy understood the pronoun, but she understood nothing beyond that.

"Ruined him?" she repeated, wholly at a loss. "Whom have you ruined, Cicily? What do you mean?"

Then, the young wife poured forth the tale of the disaster she had all unwittingly wrought in the affairs of her husband. She explained her high hopes of saving a dangerous situation by means of her own influence over the women, who, in turn, controlled the leaders among the workmen in the factory. Cicily was painfully aware of the mischief that must result from the refusal of the Civitas Society to welcome into its sacred circle the three candidates whom she had proposed. She knew the sensitiveness of these women, knew that they would bitterly resent the slight thus put upon them. Where she had meant to bind their friendship for her, she had succeeded only in creating a situation by which they might well come to detest her for having subjected them to needless humiliation. With their hostility aroused against her, they would throw their influence, which she believed dominant, to persuade the men against any concessions in favor of their employer. With a full perception of the catastrophe in which she had so innocently become involved, the wife hurriedly recounted the facts to her aunt, bewailing the evil destiny that had worked such dire havoc with her schemes for good.

"Well, you did what you could," Mrs. Delancy suggested consolingly, when at last the melancholy recital was ended.

"And I failed!" came the retort, in a voice of misery.

Certain utterances of the girl on a former occasion had rankled in the bosom of the old lady, perhaps because she perceived a certain element of justice in them, and by so much a measure of dereliction on her own part in the regulating of affairs between herself and her husband. Now, despite the kindliness of her nature and her real sympathy for the suffering of the niece who knelt at her knees, she could not forbear a mild reproof:

"Well, Cicily," she said gently, "it all comes of a woman fooling with business. Why, if you'd only been content to work for the heathen—"

"I've just finished with the heathen!" was the quick interruption.

"Well, my dear," Mrs. Delancy commented drily, "if you'd only work for the far-off heathen, you'd find it much more satisfactory. You might not do any good, to be sure; but, anyhow, the bad results wouldn't affect you."

Cicily got to her feet, without making any reply, and went to the mirror at one end of the drawing-room. There, she busied herself after the feminine fashion with concealing the more apparent ravages made by her weeping. When she came back to face her aunt again, she was her usual charming self, save for a lack of color in her cheeks, and a portentous gravity in the drooping of the mouth.... Happily, she was not of the majority, whose noses bloom redly when watered with tears.

"And now," she said, desolately, "I've got to tell them!" She nodded toward the withdrawing-room, where the three candidates were waiting; and Mrs. Delancy understood.

"Why don't you write it to them?" she advised. "Whenever I have anything uncomfortable to tell anyone, I always write it. Then, I let your Uncle Jim read the reply.... It's so much more satisfactory that way, and, you know, he can say right out what I don't dare even to think."

But Cicily had courage and a conscience. She felt that she must not shirk the consequences to herself of her own indiscretion.

"No, I'll tell them," she declared resolutely; but her heart was sick within her at contemplation of the scene that waited.

Fortunately, perhaps, small time was given Cicily for dread anticipations. Hardly had she ceased speaking when the door into the withdrawing-room was cautiously opened, and the face of Mrs. McMahon was made visible to the two women who had faced about at sound of the knob turning. On perceiving that the room was empty save for the hostess and Mrs. Delancy, the Irishwoman threw the door wide, and came forward.

"Faith, it was so quiet I was sure they'd gone," she announced, with manifest pride in her deductive powers. There was, too, a general air of elation in the woman's manner of carriage that struck a chill to Cicily's heart. And the cold of it deepened as Mrs. Schmidt and Sadie Ferguson followed into the drawing-room, each evidently in a state of exaltation. The three ranged themselves in rude dignity before their hostess. Mrs. McMahon constituted herself the spokeswoman.

"Well," she inquired genially, "now that we're members of the club, what is it you'd be after having us to do?"

An interval of silence followed, under the influence of which the three waiting candidates seemed visibly to droop, as if by a subtle instinct they began to apprehend misfortune. When, finally, Cicily spoke, it was in a colorless voice:

"I'm afraid there is nothing that any of us can do, now." The three started, and exchanged glances in which was dawning alarm, "I mean," the unhappy hostess went on, making her confession of failure by a mighty effort of will, "that—that the election did not go as I had expected it to."

Again, there was a painful silence, in which Sadie fidgeted and Mrs. Schmidt seemed to grow more shrunken and faded than before. Mrs. McMahon alone stood unmovingly erect, stiffly pugnacious on the instant.

"So, that's it!" she exclaimed, at last. Her big voice was raucous with anger. "Sure, then, and we're not members, at all!"

As the bald truth was thus made known to Sadie, she flared into complete forgetfulness of the ideal deportment of her heroines.

"Them cats turn us down!" she screeched.

Mrs. Schmidt uttered no word, for she was by nature given to profound silences, almost unbroken for days. Perhaps, she believed the garrulity of her husband ample for the entire family. Nevertheless, in this critical moment, Mrs. Schmidt opened her mouth repeatedly, like a fish out of water, as if she were striving her utmost to speak.

"And—and," Cicily added weakly, "I'm awfully sorry."

"Sure, and you don't need to trouble yourself, Mrs. Hamilton," the Irishwoman declared, viciously. "The likes of us know how you rich people have a habit of bringing us into your parlors to make fun for their friends. You come to our homes, and we treated you like a lady. Faith, now we come here, and you treat us like monkeys—that's all the difference. We're much obliged to you for the lesson. Sure, and we won't bother you again, not a bit of it. And we'll be pleased if you'll treat us the same.... Good-day to you, Mrs. Hamilton." The irate woman bobbed her head energetically at her hostess, and strode toward the doorway into the hall. But she halted for a moment as Cicily addressed her impetuously.

"Mrs. McMahon, you must listen to me! I had no idea that this would turn out as it did. I have been your friend—I am your friend. When the club refused to admit you, I resigned from the club. There is nothing more that I can do. Oh, I am so sorry that it all occurred!"

"Faith, we'll take your explanation for all it's worth," was the wrathful woman's comment, uttered with scorn. She was too deeply hurt to be solaced by explanations that did not alter the shameful fact one whit. She turned again toward the doorway, only to be halted by the appearance there of her husband, accompanied by Schmidt and Ferguson.

McMahon paused just within the room, and stood rubbing his hands, and grinning jovially, his round face aglow with satisfaction. He addressed his wife banteringly, evidently in high good spirits:

"Faith, Katy McMahon," he exclaimed, "but you're looking proud the day! Sure, now, I'll have the automobile to take us all up to Sherry's in just a minute, when we've done talking with Mr. Hamilton. Bedad, with our wives and daughters moving in such elegant society and members of such a grand club with the boss's wife, we wouldn't dare take them any less place at all!"

"It's a bad mind-reader you are!" fairly shouted the outraged wife. Sadie added something unintelligible, it was so rapidly uttered and so venomously hissed. Even Mrs. Schmidt displayed every symptom of speech save sound.

"What's the matter, Sadie?" Ferguson demanded, not unkindly, as he observed the expression on his daughter's face. "Wasn't your false hair the right shade? I'm sorry, if it ain't, because I don't see as how I can buy you any more with this ten per cent. cut we're taking."

Instantly, Cicily aroused to new hope. She moved a stop forward, her hands up-raised in eagerness. A glow of color burned in either cheek, and her eyes sparkled again.

"Oh," she questioned tensely, "then you're not going to strike—you'll take the cut?"

It was Schmidt who answered, beaming happily on his hostess.

"Strike? Ah, no! When you make friends with our wives, and Mr. Hamilton, he tells us the truth just like one man with another, we appreciate it, yes; we stand by and help, yes!"

"Schmidt's right," Ferguson added. "Mr. Hamilton and you, ma'am, are human. So, we've decided to stick it out for a while, anyhow."

McMahon, too, yielded his tribute of commendation.

"Yes, Mrs. Hamilton," he said seriously, "there's one thing that the bosses generally don't understand; but the men always appreciate it when the boss, and the boss's wife, too, are on the level."

To the amazement of everyone, Mrs. Schmidt broke into speech; find that outburst was like the eruction of Krakatao in its unexpectedness, its suddenness, its overwhelming virulence.

"Yes, yes, yes," she clamored, addressing her hapless husband, who stood appalled before the attack, "you are one big, fat fool! You always were. You are in love with her—no? You let her bring your wife here, make her for a joke to her rich friends, let her get insults. They laugh and make fun of me, Frieda Schmidt, your wife; and then, when they have had the good laugh, they say: 'What do you think we want of you? You are not like us. We are grand ladies: you are a working woman. Get out! Get out! We have had our laugh at you. Now, go! We are through; we are tired of you. It was very good of Mrs. Hamilton to bring you here for us to laugh at; but it is over. Get out!'... And then you come and thank her because she insults your wife, insults your name; and you take less wages from her husband because she insults your name and me. If you take that cut, you are not my man—never with me no more!" With the last words, she darted from the room, and a moment later the street-door slammed violently behind her.

"Good for Frieda!" Mrs. McMahon applauded. "When she does talk, sure she says something.... You heard her, Mike McMahon? Well, what she said, them's my sentiments. You know what she did now." A jerk of the head indicated the wretched hostess. "She pretended to ask us to join a club. She brought us here to insult us, to make fun of us. She made us the laughing-stock of Morton and Carrington's wives. Do you hear that? Morton and Carrington! Put the names of them in your pipe and smoke it. Mike McMahon, listen to what I'm telling you. If you take a cut from them that insult your wife, you can forget to come home for good, my bucco." In her turn, the Irishwoman stalked out of the room and from the house with a tread of heavy dignity.

"That goes with me, Pop!" Sadie declared, as she flounced out.

"It's all been a terrible mistake," Cicily ventured to the three men who stood regarding her with sullen faces and baleful eyes after the revelations that had just been made.

"I'm thinking you're right," McMahon agreed. There was something sinister in his voice. "But it's us that made the mistake. We thought the boss and his wife could be on the level with us. What a bunch of damn fools we were!" And his two confrères nodded gloomy assent.

It was at this most unpropitious moment that Hamilton came briskly into the room. He stopped short in the doorway, at sight of the three men of the committee, who turned to face him.

"Well, boys," he exclaimed briskly, "have you decided?" The men nodded without speaking. "Well?"

"I'll do the talking," Ferguson said, holding up a hand to check Schmidt. "We've decided, Mr. Hamilton. We're going to strike. We'll make you come to terms, or we'll bust you if we can."

Hamilton's face hardened, and he squared his shoulders.

"I suppose you know what you're up against?" he questioned harshly.

"Yes, we've just found out," Ferguson retorted, with gusty rage. "We'd been thinking that you were on the level—you and your wife, too. We swallowed that funny story of your being crushed by the trust. Oh, we were suckers, all right. We were suckers for fair! We were going to fall for it. We were going take your cut. And then your wife brings our wives and daughters here, pretending she's going to put them in her club—brings them here to make a laugh for Morton and Carrington's wives. Yes, Morton and Carrington, the very men you say are crushing you, your enemies! Oh, your enemies are all right! Do you think we are fools? No, to hell with you!" The furious man's voice rose to a shriek with the last words. He whirled, and made for the door, and the other two followed him.

"One minute," Hamilton called. "You needn't go back to the works. We close down in ten minutes. Come back to see me when you are hungry." He stood motionless as the men passed silently out, and until he heard the sound of the street-door closing behind them. Then, he turned to Cicily, who had waited pallid and shaken, her eyes downcast, her hands clasped distressedly. His voice, as he spoke, was not softened; even, it was harder than before. "You see what you have done," he said simply. "This settles it. I'm going into a big fight. I can't be handicapped. For the future, you will stay where you belong. You will confine your activities to the house, where they will be less dangerous, let us hope—less fatal!" Without awaiting any reply, he wheeled, and strode from the room.

CHAPTER XII

Cicily sent word of a severe headache, and did not appear at the dinner-table that night, nor did she see her husband during the evening. She retired to her bed-chamber at an early hour, but not to sleep. Instead, she abandoned herself to torturing reflections on the malevolent predicament into which she had been brought. She did not attempt to disguise from herself the hideous fact that her own precipitancy of action in the matter of the candidates for the club had been the primary cause of the peril that now beset her husband's business prosperity by reason of the strike thus induced. She bewailed the impetuous character of her emotions, which had so evilly led her into an action fraught with such dire consequences. She had no regret for the motives that had impelled her, but she was profoundly sorrowful over the thoughtless haste with which she had entered on a course of more than doubtful expediency. Her one relief was in a reiteration that she would, that she must, find some way by which to make amends for the catastrophe she had so ingenuously engineered. To the discovery of a method for retrieving her error, she gave her mind with an almost frenzied concentration; but the effort was fruitless. Cudgel her wearied brain as she would, it could not make pace to the goal she sought. When, after a sleepless night, she rose, it was with the maze of disaster still unthreaded. Her usual ingenuity of resource was become impotent. Raging against her own supineness, she was yet forced into ignoble inactivity.

Cicily learned that her husband had breakfasted early, and had left the house, without any message to her, or any statement as to when he might return. The sight of food sickened her, but she managed to drink a cup of coffee, which put a little heart into her after the wearing hours of the night. A turn around the Park and along the Drive still further quickened her spirits; but the day passed without any flash of inspiration as to a means for undoing the ill she had wrought. She made a toilette for dinner by a brave effort. Yet, she might have spared her pains, for Hamilton did not appear. She idled through the meal with as much cheeriness of demeanor as she could summon for the benefit of the servants. Afterward, she sought the seclusion of her boudoir, leaving word that she should be notified immediately in the event of her husband's return.

In the meantime, Hamilton himself had opportunity for meditation, and this had softened his mood to some degree. He admitted to himself that her interest in the wives of his workmen had been the prime factor in their determination to endure a temporary cut in the wage-scale without striking. To be sure, his own attitude of confidential intercourse with the leaders in stating his position frankly had had its influence; but he did not for a moment believe that this alone would have sufficed to bend the men to his will. No, it had been the happy effect of his wife's intimate association on terms of equality with the women that had been the chief factor in creating a sentiment of sympathy for him to the extent of coöperation. Without her work in his behalf, the men would certainly have struck. Now, since her mistake in judgment had been the immediate cause of the strike, in justice she could hardly be held guilty of more than an act of folly. Essentially, the final situation was what it would have been without any intervention whatsoever on her part. In going over the succession of events logically and calmly, Hamilton came to the decision that he would absolve his wife from any real guilt in the affair. He even felt a half-hearted kindliness toward her for her blundering good-will. But he was none the less resolved that he would tolerate no further injection of this charming feminine personality into his business concerns. The wife must mind her own business—the home—and that alone; she must have no part in his.... It was in this mood that he returned to his house late in the evening, and shut himself into the study. There, presently, Cicily came, seeking him.

The bride was very beautiful to-night, with a touch of sadness in her expression that gave her a new spirituelle charm. She had chosen a black gown as becoming the melancholy of the time, but its austere lines, without any touch of adornment, only brought into full relief the exquisite outlines of the slenderly rounded form, and served to emphasize the creamy whiteness of a complexion that was flawless. There was hardly a glimpse of rose in the ivory curve of the cheeks, but there was no lessening of the bending scarlet in the lips and the amber eyes were luminous even beyond their wont, as their gentle radiance shone forth above the dark circles traced by a sleepless night.

Hamilton turned a little as the door opened. He regarded his wife quizzically as she walked forward with a step of native grace, now grown a trifle languid from the weight on her spirit. He did not speak, however, until she had seated herself in the chair facing his. Then, when at last she looked up, and her somber gaze encountered his, he spoke lightly:

"Cicily, my dear, I think you are well rid of that coterie of cats."

"Why, how did you know?" Cicily questioned, in some astonishment as to his knowledge of her break with the members of the Civitas Society.

"Oh, in a very simple way. Aunt Emma told Uncle Jim, and Uncle Jim told me," Then, out of the kindness of his heart, the young husband went on speaking in such wise, according to his best judgment, as should console the very apparent misery of his wife. "My dear," he said gently, "I want you to know that I don't really blame you for this wretched strike. I'd have had it on my hands just the same, if you'd never had a finger in the pie. So, don't go grieving over something that can't be helped. And, of course, I give you all credit for the very best of intentions in the matter. Only—" he broke off discreetly; but the discretion had come too late.

"Only what?" Cicily questioned, quietly. There was something ominous in the quiet, and this the man realized.

Nevertheless, Hamilton was not one to shirk that which he deemed his duty. So, now, he answered lucidly with just what was in his mind as to the future relations between them, although he understood sufficiently well the ambitions of the woman before him to know that he must wound her deeply.

"Sweetheart," he said softly, "I don't wish to grieve you in any way. Yet, I must insist calmly now on what I said yesterday in the heat of anger. You must attend to your duty in the home. It is for me, and for me alone, to conduct matters of business outside. Can you not understand that you are by nature and training utterly incompetent for the rôle you seek to play? Business aptitude is not a thing to be picked up in an instant, haphazard, at the wish of anyone. It is something acquired by long striving and experience. The man has it in greater or less degree, as the result of generations of the work; he inherits an aptitude; he develops it by systematic training. Feminine intuition cannot give you a substitute for the practical needs of business. So, my dear, I beg you to be reasonable. You must not meddle further in my affairs. But, don't, for heaven's sake, be melancholy over it. I love you, my dear, and I want you to be happy. You will be, if only you can get the right point of view. Try! Won't you, dear?" As he finished speaking with this appeal, Hamilton leaned forward anxiously, pleadingly. Deep down in his heart he felt a glow of pride over the mildness and the reasonableness with which he had presented the case in its true light to this irrational, dear creature.

For a long minute, Cicily vouchsafed no answer, although she felt the intensity of his gaze fixed upon her. She remained motionless, leaning back in the chair, her taper fingers loosely clasped on her lap, her eyes downcast, as one absorbed in earnest, yet not disquieting, thought. Finally, however, she raised her head slowly, and her gaze met that of her husband fairly. It seemed to him that perhaps the faint touch of color in her cheeks had grown a little brighter, but of this he could not be sure. Otherwise, certainly, she betrayed no sign of particular emotion; whereat he rejoiced, since he knew from experience that her temperament might manifest tumultuously on occasion.

"Then, it's come," she said at last, in a low voice. Again, her eyes were downcast, and she rested there, to all appearance, tranquilly indifferent.

Hamilton stirred uneasily. This was not what he had expected, and he found himself unprepared for the emergency.

"If you mean that common-sense has come," he remarked grimly, "I beg to tell you that it has, and that it has come to stay!"

The wife spoke again, rather languidly, without troubling to raise her eyes.

"You mean that you are going to push me back, that you are going to shut me out of your life totally—out of your big, whole, full life? You mean that, for the future, you are going to treat me as a doll, as a plaything with which to amuse yourself when you chance to be tired and in a mood for such diversion—in fact, as other men of the average sort treat their wives? You have told your side of it. Now, I'm going to tell you mine. And I'm going to ask you not to decide too hastily. Think over the matter carefully, I beg of you. For, you see, it involves our whole future, yours and mine.... Charles, once you yielded to my wishes. You took me in. You let me help you."

"Yes," exclaimed Hamilton, in exasperation of spirit. "And you made a mess of things all round!" He shook his head emphatically. "No, Cicily; I tell you, no!"

"Charles, wait!" the wife commanded, raising her eyes, and straightening her form in sudden animation. "Take my money—take everything that I have. Throw it away, if you want to. Use it in your business, if it will help the least bit. Do whatever you please—only, don't shut me out. Tell me everything. Teach me something of your knowledge concerning these things. Let me share as much as I can. You direct, of course. I'll only do what you wish me to do. But don't drive me away from you." She paused, leaned farther forward, and went on speaking in a tone of deepest seriousness: "If we part this way now, if I am to cease from any interest in your affairs, and you go on alone, why, then, I'll never have you again. I know that for the truth. That's why I am pleading like this. Once, I demanded it as a right; now, I beg it as a favor. Here is the choice, Charles. You can't be as Uncle Jim is, simply because I won't be like Aunt Emma in this matter. If you shut me out now, I'll shut you out—for good!"

"Good God! was there ever such a woman!" Hamilton cried, in desperation. "Why, if I were to take you in, within two weeks you'd be down there, helping the families of the strikers. You told me that, yourself."

"Would you have me see them starve, Charles, when I had the means for their relief?" came the undaunted retort.

"That does settle it!" Hamilton exclaimed, with angry vehemence. It came to him in this instant that all his reasonableness and gentleness were futile when opposed to the unfeminine ambition of his girl wife. Temper had him in its clutch, and he yielded blindly to its guidance. "I'm your husband, Cicily," he announced, dictatorially. "Please, understand that, from now on, I direct the affairs of this family. There can be no happiness in a house without head— only bother and worry and confusion. From now on, I direct. I'm the head of this house.... I have a big fight on. I intend that you shall be loyal. I mean that you shall be faithful to me straight through."

"You demand this?" The woman's voice was like ice.

"Yes," the husband replied, roughly. "I demand that you take your proper place, the place of a wife in her husband's home; and that you stay there, doing as I tell you. And, in this strike, you keep your hands off. This is what you must do, as long as I am your husband." The man's eyes were masterful; his jaw was thrust forward.

"Well, if that's the sort of man you are, I won't have you for a husband," Cicily declared, quietly. There was an air of aloofness about her that was more disturbing than had been a display of passion. "If that's your idea of marriage, we'd be better apart, for it isn't mine. No, you're not my husband," She stood up, slowly drew the wedding-ring from her finger, and laid it on the table.

"Cicily!" Hamilton cried, aghast, as she turned away.

She did not pause until she was come to the door. But, there, she faced about for a final utterance.

"No, I won't have you for a husband," was her ultimatum.... "And yet, I think that I'll teach you a lesson. I have a fancy to save you—in spite of yourself!" And, leaving Hamilton to ponder these astounding words, she went forth from the room.

CHAPTER XIII

The week that followed was to Cicily the most strenuous and the most exciting that she had ever experienced in the brief span of her years. She steadfastly maintained her pose as a woman who had renounced her husband; yet, she remained in that husband's house, with a sublime disregard for the inconsistency of her conduct. She studiously avoided any discussion, of the status she had established. What her future course would be was left wholly to conjecture. She presided at the table with inimitable grace and self-possession, taking care to treat her husband with every consideration, but always with a trace of formality that was significant of the changed relation. Hamilton, on his part, was inclined to regard his wife's dramatic renunciation of him as a passing whim, which it were wiser to ignore until such time as it should have worn itself out. In the meantime, he was so much absorbed by the struggle over his business difficulties that, he had little time or disposition to make researches into feminine psychology, even that of his wife. He had an optimistic theory that, in the end, his domestic troubles would adjust themselves by some process of natural evolution. He was confident, too, that his assertion of mastery must eventually be accepted by his wife. So, he smiled pleasantly on Cicily, when he was not too busy to notice her presence, and betimes he felt the little packet that he carried in the inner pocket of his waistcoat, and was fondly content, wondering when the dear girl would again slip the bond of servitude willingly on the finger whence she had removed it with such magnificent disdain.

It was that wedding-ring, thus cherished by Hamilton, which caused the wife more concern than aught else in her domestic entanglement. She had regarded the symbol as something splendidly sacred, and she now bitterly regretted the impulse that had led her to discard it so needlessly. Indeed, the very night on which she defied her husband, she had crept down to the library when all the house was quiet, and had there made sure that it was not still lying disregarded on the table where she had cast it down in resentment. Now, she hoped and believed that her husband had locked it away in some drawer where at least it would be safe. Only, she wished that she had saved it as a souvenir of mingled happiness and sorrow.

Apart from this matter of the ring, Cicily had no remorse. She regretted the course of action thrust on her by malign fate, but her conscience was clear of reproach. Perhaps, in some subtle, unconfessed recess of her heart, she nourished a hope that ultimately joy would return to her life. But her openly expressed conviction to herself was that she was done with the life of love. Yet, a curious personal ambition urged her on to make good the declaration to her husband that she would save him in spite of himself. To this end, she bent all her energies. As she reflected on the circumstances under which she had so ignominiously failed, she decided that she must have recourse again to the means by which she had so nearly attained success in her plans for her husband's welfare, only to fail miserably on account of the obstinacy of the Civitas Society. So, she sought out the women whom she had unhappily offered as candidates to the club, and set herself with all the art that was in her to win back their favor. She was sure that by alliance with them she could mold circumstance to her will, and ultimately triumph gloriously over the erring man who had flouted her ambition to help in a business struggle.

Cicily made a full confession of her marital disaster to Mrs. Delancy, who by turns scolded and cried over the wilful girl. The old lady disapproved strongly of her niece's conduct, which was without any excuse whatsoever according to her own notions of conventional requirements. But, since she loved this child whom she had mothered, she forgave her, and by degrees came to feel a certain sympathy for her, which reacted mildly in her own attitude toward her husband.... It was on one of her visits to her aunt that Cicily encountered Mr. Delancy, who was already aware of the unfortunate position of affairs, and now felt himself called on to protest. He expressed himself with some severity, and concluded with a hope that she was not determined to persevere in her folly.

"I was never more determined in my whole life, Uncle Jim," was the emphatic answer.

Mr. Delancy resisted a temptation to snatch up one of the teacups from the exquisite Sèvres service over which his wife and his niece were sitting, and to hurl it into the fireplace, for the sake of relieving his choler. He refrained from any overt act, however, by a great effort of will, and perforce contented himself with an explicit statement of his opinion:

"You were never more bull-headed in your life," he snorted, stopping short in his agitated pacing of the drawing-room, to face his niece with a scowl; "and that's saying a great deal—a very great deal!"

"James!" Mrs. Delancy exclaimed, in mild remonstrance.

But Cicily was not to be suppressed by this man who typified the evils against which she had fought.

"Would you have me give up my principles?" she questioned, scornfully.

Once again, Mr. Delancy snorted contemptuously.

"You haven't got any principles," he declared, baldly. "No woman has."

At this brutal statement on the part of her husband, Mrs. Delancy stiffened, and an exclamation of shocked amazement burst from her. Cicily smiled cynically, as she addressed her aunt:

"Well, Aunt Emma," she said amusedly, "you see now what your attitude has led to. You began with no backbone. So, now, you have no principles. Oh, you nice, sweet-faced, gray-headed, deceiving old-lady reprobate, you!"

But Mrs. Delancy refused to see any element of humor in the situation. Indeed, she was on the verge of tears over the wantonly injurious statement made by the husband whom she had cherished for a lifetime.

"James, how could you!" she cried out, in a voice broken by emotion. "To say such things to your wife—oh!"

Too late, the irascible husband realized that he had committed a serious fault, had in fact been guilty of a gross injustice, which was hardly less than an insult, to the woman whom he thoroughly respected.

"Emma—" he began, appealingly.

But Mrs. Delancy had changed in an instant from tearful reproach to righteous indignation.

"No, don't speak to me!" she commanded; and she deliberately turned her back on the culprit.

Under the goad of this treatment, Delancy addressed his niece in a tone that was almost ferocious.

"So," he snarled, "not content with breaking up your own home, you'd try to ruin mine, would you! You should apologize to your Aunt Emma, at once."

"Dear Auntie," Cicily exclaimed without a moment's hesitation, in a voice of contrition, "I beg you to let me apologize to you very humbly for what Uncle James said."

"What the—!" stormed the badgered old gentleman. "Now, look here, Cicily. You think you're very smart. But do you know what your attitude has led to?—Scandal!"

Mrs. Delancy forgot for the moment her own subject for complaint.

"Yes," she agreed, turning to her niece, "it's a scandal to live in a house with a strange man—you know, that's what you yourself called Charles."

"It's a worse scandal," Delancy amended, "not to live with him."

"Oh, I see," Cicily remarked, meditatively. "I must have a chaperon. But, on the other hand, now, Charles is, or rather he was, my husband. That seems, somehow, to make a difference. At least, we are well acquainted, although strangers at present, in a sense. And, besides, I have the kindliest feeling for Charles, and that's more than lots of women have for their husbands. As to that, you know, since he's not my husband now, there is really no reason why I should not have the very kindliest of feelings for him."

"Well, you claim to renounce your husband," Delancy argued angrily, "and yet you continue to live with him in the same house. It's a monstrous state of affairs. Will you tell me, please, madam, when this scandalous situation is to end?"

"Would you have me desert Charles in a crisis?" Cicily demanded, haughtily. "No, I'll give no one an opportunity to accuse me of desertion in the face of the enemy."

"Oh, Lord!" Delancy exclaimed; and his tone was eloquent. "Oh, no, you haven't deserted him!"

"I don't see what that has to do with it," Cicily objected, flushing painfully. "Charles and I have merely—that is, we've—broken off diplomatic relations."

At this extraordinary statement of the case, Mrs. Delancy, in her turn, flushed a dainty pink, which was wondrously becoming to her waxen cheeks, not unduly wrinkled despite her burden of years. Delancy himself forgot indignation for the moment, and laughed outright, as he regarded his wife to observe the manner in which she received the surprising information. His eyes took on a kindlier expression as he saw the change that gave her a wondrously younger look, and a rush of memories caused him to smile reminiscently, half-sadly, half-tenderly. The effect on him was apparent in the pleasanter voice with which he next addressed his niece, playfully:

"My, my! She'd be sending him home to his mother, I expect, if only he had a mother."

Cicily, still suffering in the throes of a painful embarrassment, retorted hotly:

"Uncle Jim, I'd just like to shake you!"

"Oh, don't mind my gray hairs," Delancy scoffed. "And, when you're done with me, you might spank your Aunt Emma."

That good woman shook her head dolorously, as the flush died from her face.

"I don't know what we're coming to," she mourned.

"Anarchy!" was her husband's prompt answer, as he mounted again on his favorite hobby. "Once women begin to believe that they have intelligence, anarchy will be the natural, the inevitable result. God never made them to think." In his excitement, he had forgotten the manner in which he had already once offended his wife.

"Then, why did God give women brains?" Cicily demanded.

"I can't waste my time in arguing with a woman," Delancy answered loftily, and, turning away, tugged superciliously at a wisp of whisker.

"That's it! Oh, yes, that's it!" Cicily exclaimed, with rising indignation. Her embarrassment had passed, but a flush remained in her cheeks, and her radiant eyes were alight with the battle-lust. "You think women haven't any intelligence. You can't waste your time arguing with them! Very well, then, I tell you that it's you who haven't the intelligence to recognize a new point of view—a new force in the world; the force of women's brains—until it shall hit you in the face. That's why I'm holding out against Charles, fighting him, to save him, to keep him from growing into a narrow-minded, hard-headed, ignorant old fossil!" The application of this explicit description was not far to seek. It was evident that Delancy took it to himself, for he, in his turn at last, colored rosily. But he did not choose to accept a personal reference, and contented himself with a bit of repartee:

"Huh, no fear! He won't live to be a fossil. His troubles will kill him off early, or I lose my guess.... So, that's your excuse for ruining him, is it?"

"I'd help him, if he'd let me," Cicily answered, sadly, forgetful of her indignation against the sex.

"You help him!" Delancy exclaimed, mockingly. "Why, you brought on the strike."

"But—" Cicily would have protested, only to be interrupted by the indignant old gentleman, who shook an accusing forefinger at her.

"You can't tell me! Yes, you did, with your impertinent interference. Huh! When women get to fooling with business, we shall all go to the dogs. Why, if it hadn't been for you and for what you did with your precious 'helping,' Charles would have had a chance to make good money. Now, Morton and Carrington are charging the independent dealers twenty-two cents a box. But for this strike, Charles might have induced those old pirates to raise their price to him a little, and let him make some money.... Help him—oh, piffle!"

"Well," Cicily declared, not a whit abashed, "if I were Charles, I'd start up again, pay wages, and sell to the independents."

The seriousness with which the young woman spoke for a moment betrayed Delancy into discussing business with one of the unintelligent sex.

"But his contracts!" he objected.

"What are contracts," Cicily interrupted serenely, "when the workmen are hungry?"

"There, Emma!" Delancy cried, in deep disgust. "Do you hear? Now, isn't that just like a woman?"

"Yes, James," Mrs. Delancy answered meekly; "I know that you're right. But, somehow, I think Cicily, too, is right."

At this paradoxical pronouncement, Delancy stared fixedly at his wife in stark amazement.

"What!" he gasped. "What! After forty years, you say that to me! You question my business judgment! Emma, you, my wife!" He struggled wildly for a few seconds to gain control of his emotions. "No," he continued bitterly; "I deserve it for forgetting myself. I beg my own pardon for mentioning a word of business to a woman.... I'm going to Charles—poor fellow!" After a long, resentful stare directed against his former ward, he marched out of the room.

"See what you've made me do!" Mrs. Delancy said accusingly to her niece, as the two were left alone together. "Why, I've actually appeared rebellious to James."

"You ought to have been so years ago," Cicily rejoined, stubbornly.

But Mrs. Delancy could only shake her head morosely in negation of this audacious idea. Then, her thoughts reverted to the young woman's doubtful position.

"How is it all going to end?" was her despondent query.

"You mean, when are Charles and I going to make public the true state of affairs? When are we going to part before the world?" The old lady nodded acquiescence. "Well, that will be when the strike is over, and Charles's business troubles are settled—not before."

"If this sort of thing keeps on," Mrs. Delancy announced, with another access of self-pity, "your Uncle Jim and I probably will be parted by that time, too!"

"Nonsense!" Cicily jeered, smitten to sudden compunction for her part in causing distress of mind to the woman whom she really loved and honored. "Why, Auntie, if you were to leave Uncle Jim, whom would he have to bully? Pooh, dear, you and he'll never part."

Again, the old lady's thoughts veered from herself.

"But, Cicily," she ventured, "you're doing your best to prolong the strike. You're actually giving those women money, I know. Yesterday, when I called to see you, I saw the stub in your chequebook, which was lying open on the desk in your boudoir. I didn't mean to pry, but I couldn't help seeing it."

"Well, I'm not letting them starve," was the unashamed admission.

"Cicily," Mrs. Delancy said, with an abrupt transition from one phase of the subject under consideration to another, "about this matter of you and Charles separating, I have a suspicion that you are very much like that highly improper young woman in the French story, who was going to live with her lover as long as the geranium lasted. And you're going to live in the house with Charles while his troubles continue. And that improper young woman used to get up in the night, every night, to water the geranium, secretly. And you are providing the strikers with food, to prolong the strike. Humph! You don't want to go." Cicily blushed a little, but attempted no reply. "You're in love with him—you know you are!"

The young wife's reserve broke down a little before the keen glance that accompanied the words.

"I—oh, I'm interested in his spiritual development," she stammered, weakly. "Anyhow," she added defensively, "he—doesn't know it!"

"Thank heaven, you're still moral!" Mrs. Delancy ejaculated, in accents of huge relief.

"I think I must be," was the low-spoken admission, "because—because I'm so unhappy!" The scarlet lips drooped to a tremulous pathos, as she went on speaking in a voice of poignant feeling. "Oh, Aunt Emma, when I see Charles so harassed, so tired, so troubled in every way, I just long to throw my arms around his neck, and to kiss all those hard lines away from his dear face, and to tell him how much I love him, and how sorry I am, and how much I want to help him."

"Heaven bless you, child!" Mrs. Delancy exclaimed, surprised and delighted. "Why don't you, then?"

"Because," came the gloomy explanation, "if I did, I'd be like you."

The old lady was not gratified by this candid defense.

"Humph! Well, you might do worse, if I do say so myself," she declared, with a toss of her head.

"Of course, you old dear," Cicily agreed, with an air of humility, "in lots and lots of ways—but—"

"You're obstinate!" came the tart rebuke. "If you're really in love with him, give in!"

"That's just the trouble," the young wife said. "Because I'm so much in love with him, I can't give in in this particular. I love him too much to be content with just the bits of him that are left over from the other things. I want a partnership. Marriage has changed since your day, Auntie. Real marriage to-day must be a partnership in all things. I must have that, a full share in my husband's life—or nothing! I tell you, there is too much of men and women swearing before God to become as one, and walking away to begin life and to live it ever after as two. It was all very well when the women had the house to keep, and didn't think; but nowadays most of them have no house to keep, and they are beginning to think."

"But," Mrs. Delancy objected, much discomposed by this tirade against matrimony as she knew it, "you're upsetting all the holy things. To look up to your husband—that's love."

"That's lonesomeness and a crick in the neck!" was the flippant denial. "My woman would stand where her brains entitle her to stand, beside her husband, looking into his eyes, working for him, working with him, being together with him straight through everything. That's love; that's real marriage!"

"Cicily," Mrs. Delancy protested, totally bemused by her niece's fiery eloquence, "I think you're wrong, but I—I feel that you're right."

"Deep down in your heart, dear," the young woman asserted with profound conviction, "you know that I'm right, because you're a real woman. The men don't know it—poor things!—but the ruling passion of a woman's life is usefulness. And isn't it much nicer to work for a husband whom you love than for the heathen?"

Before her aunt could frame an adequate answer to this very pertinent inquiry, Cicily sprung up, with the graceful animation that was usual with her.

"And, now, I must hurry home," she announced, "to receive Mrs. McMahon and Mrs. Schmidt and Sadie Ferguson, who are coming to call."

"Merciful providence!" Mrs. Delancy ejaculated, in genuine horror. "You don't mean to tell me that those women come to your house now?"

"Oh, yes," was the nonchalant assent. "Why shouldn't they? You know, we're friends again now. I've organized them into a club."

"Well, I do not think it's at all proper," the old lady said, with severe decisiveness.

But Cicily only laughed under the reproof, bestowed a hasty kiss on her aunt's cheek, and swept buoyantly from the room.

CHAPTER XIV

When Mrs. McMahon, Mrs. Schmidt and Miss Ferguson were ushered into the drawing-room of the Hamilton house, Cicily was there, ready to welcome her guests warmly.

"And how is Madam President of our club?" she said with a delightful assumption of deference to Mrs. McMahon, who bridled and simpered in proud happiness over this recognition of the honor she enjoyed.

"Indeed, she's as proud as a peacock, that she is," she avowed candidly. "And, if you noticed, Mrs. Hamilton, I didn't so much as say how do you do to the man at the door, as I always have before, nor even so much as look at him.... For such is the high-society way of it, they're after telling me."

Cicily smiled, and then addressed Sadie with a like cordiality.

"Everything is shipshape, Miss Secretary?" she inquired.

"This club could go ten rounds without turning a hair," was the spirited reply. Then, the ambitious girl recalled her most esteemed author, and paraphrased her statement: "I mean, every thing is really quite splendid."

Mrs. Schmidt, too, smiled in appreciation, although without committing herself to words, when she was addressed as Madam Vice-President. Then, after all were seated, the Irishwoman delivered herself of a message of gratitude.

"Mrs. Hamilton," she said, and her great, round face was very kindly, "we want to thank you here and now for that last cheque. You'll be glad to know that Murphy's babies are fine and dandy; and those Dagos—you know, the ones in the sixth floor front in Sadie's house—faith, the wife come home from the hospital last night looking just grand."

"And say, Mrs. Hamilton," Sadie interrupted enthusiastically, again forgetful of niceties in diction by reason of her excess of feeling, "maybe you ain't in strong with that bunch! They were all singing and praying for you all last night to beat the band. They made so much fuss Pop had to go up with a club, and threaten to bust some heads in before anybody could get to sleep in the house. Of course, father didn't understand. He heard them say something about Hamilton, and guessed they might be some sort of poor connection of the boss."

Cicily, pleased by this information as to the gratitude of those whom she had sought to serve, yet tried to change the subject for modesty's sake.

"You, Mrs. McMahon," she directed briskly, "must be in charge. You must let me know about the sick ones and the hungry ones, and then I'll see what can be done."

"'Deed, and I will that," was the eager response. Then, the Irishwoman shook her huge head admiringly. "Sure, when the women get the votes, you'll be elected alderman from the ward." But, as Cicily would have laughingly protested against this arrant flattery, a sudden thought came to the President of the new club, and she spoke with an increase of seriousness: "And, oh, I was forgetting one thing! What do you think now, Mrs. Hamilton? Carrington's men have been around!" In answer to her hostess's look of bewildered inquiry, she explained the significance of the fact: "Yes, Carrington—bad luck to him!—is getting ready to start another factory, they say; and, so, he wanted to see how many of the boys he could get." Cicily uttered an exclamation of astonishment, mingled with alarm, at the news. "Yes, ma'am. I was talking to Mike McMahon, and telling him that, after all, I thought Mr. Hamilton was on the level, and that it would be a good thing to take the cut for a little while. And, then, he got mad, and he blurted out the whole thing to me. It's Tim Doolin, him what used to work in the Hamilton factory, and was discharged, and so went over to Carrington's. He's come around as a sounder. He's been advancing the boys a little on the side, and promising them good jobs and steady wages, if they'll hold out until Carrington is ready to use them at his place." The Amazon, who had raced through her narrative, paused, panting for breath.

Cicily was tense in her chair, with her cheeks flaming indignation, her golden eyes darkened with excitement.

"So," she exclaimed fiercely, "that's the way they are fighting! Shameful!"

Cicily was in the throes of a righteous wrath. Unaccustomed to the sharp practices that are endured almost without rebuke in the world of business affairs, this revelation of trickery on the part of her husband's enemies filled her with a disgusted horror. There was in the girl-wife a strong quality of the protecting maternal love in her attitude toward her husband. It was in obedience to its impelling force that she had followed so steadfastly her ambition to help him in his business, to be his partner. It was the dominance of this feeling that had caused her to stay on in her husband's house to comfort him, and if possible to save him, in the time of his tribulation. So, now, this phase of character caused her to resent as something unspeakably vile the machinations just revealed to her. There and then, she uttered a silent vow to worst these sinister foes by fair means or by foul. Her will commanded their undoing, no matter how unscrupulous the method; and conscience voiced no protest.

A movement of expectancy among the three visitors aroused Cicily from the fit of abstraction into which she had fallen, and on which the others had not ventured to obtrude themselves. She looked up, and then, following the direction of her guests' gaze, turned to see her husband, standing motionless just within the doorway of the drawing-room. He was staring with obvious amazement at the trio of women in his wife's company. Moreover, it was easy to judge from the expression on his face, with the brows drawn and the mouth set sternly, that his amazement was not builded on pleasure.... Cicily immediately rose, forgetful for the moment of her plans for vengeance against the plotters, and went forward with a pleased smile. She was well aware that her husband would not regard this visitation with equanimity, but she hoped to prevent any overt act on his part that might fatally antagonize these women, whose good will she had struggled so hard to regain for his sake. So, she faced him with an air of happy self-confidence, and spoke with the most musical cadences of her voice, the while the caress of her eyes sought to beguile the frown from his face.

"Charles, you know Mrs. McMahon, and Mrs. Schmidt, and Miss Ferguson."

"Yes, I know them," came the uncompromising answer. The grimness of his face did not relax. He had had a day of tedious worries, and the sight of the women here in his own home exasperated him almost beyond the point of endurance. "An unexpected pleasure!" he added, with an inflection that was unmistakable.

"Oh, we didn't come to see you, Mr. Hamilton," Sadie declared resentfully, in answer to that inflection. "We came to see your wife."

"These are the officers of our new woman's club," Cicily interposed, hastily. "Do sit down for a moment, Charles." She returned to her own chair; but Hamilton made no movement to obey her request. Instead, he addressed the visitors in a tone even more unpleasant than that which he had used hitherto.

"Oh, you came to get something from Mrs. Hamilton," he sneered.

"Indeed, and we did not!" the Irishwoman retorted roughly, furious at the insinuation. But her anger melted as she caught Cicily's pleading eyes. There was a grateful softness in the brogue as she added: "Sure, she's given too much already, and that's the truth."

There was no hint of relaxing in the tense severity of Hamilton's face, as he replied, without a glance toward his wife:

"So, Mrs. Hamilton has been helping the wives of the men?"

"'Tis that same she's been doing—the saints preserve her!" Mrs. McMahon answered, with pious fervor. "Faith, if the women could vote, it's president they'd make her, so it is."

Cicily could not resist a temptation to appeal.

"Charles," she urged, "if only you'll have a little patience, you'll find that they can be of service—of great service!"

Still, Hamilton ignored his wife utterly, while he addressed the three women impersonally.

"I did not know that the men were in the habit of using their wives in a strike like this." His manner was designedly offensive.

Again, it was Sadie who was first to retort, which she did with a manner that aped his own insolence.

"Well, if Mrs. Hamilton can butt into it, it's a cinch we can!"

The man's face darkened with wrath. His voice, when he spoke, sounded dangerously low and controlled.

"Mrs. Hamilton has nothing whatever to do with my business affairs," he declared, explicitly. "She has nothing whatever to do with this strike. If you women come from the men, go back and tell them that I'm not dealing with women—neither now nor in the future. If they want anything at any time, let them come for it themselves."

"Can you beat it?" Sadie demanded wonderingly, of the universe at large.

But the Irishwoman took it on herself to answer, with an explicitness equal to Hamilton's own:

"Faith, and we didn't come to see you, as you know very well, I'm thinking. If it wasn't for Mrs. Hamilton—God bless her—we wouldn't be here at all.... And 'tis sorry I am we are."

"Then, you'd better go, and relieve your feelings," was the tart rejoinder. "And you will please remember one thing: Mrs. Hamilton has absolutely no influence of any kind in this strike. I do not know in the least what she may have been doing; but, whatever it is, it's entirely apart from me."

"Charles, please—" Cicily would have protested. It seemed to her a vicious violation of good taste thus to air their marital disagreements in the presence of others. There was a perilous fire in the golden eyes; but Hamilton had no heed just now for niceties of conduct. He went on speaking, ruthlessly breaking in on his wife's attempted plea:

"Whatever Mrs. Hamilton has accomplished has been done without my consent and with her own money—entirely apart from me.... Good-day!"

Now, at last, Hamilton moved from the position he had steadily maintained before the doorway. He stepped to one side, and bowed formally to the three women, who rose promptly as they realized the significance of his action. Cicily, too, stood up, wordless in her suffering. For the moment, at least, her indomitable spirit was overwhelmed by this crowning misfortune, and she felt all her ambition hopelessly baffled. Through this last catastrophe, her benevolent scheming must be brought to nought. It was impossible for her to believe that these women, on whose support she had relied for so much that was vital to her plans, could remain loyal to her after the gross insult to which they had been subjected in her own house. She realized that, deprived of their aid, she could not hope to cope with the situation that threatened ruin to the man whom she loved. In that instant of disaster, she hated her husband as much as she loved him, for his folly had destroyed all the structure of safety that her devotion had builded. So, she stood silent, watching the discarded guests as they walked toward the door. Her slender form was drawn to its full height; the scarlet lips were set tensely; the clear gold of her eyes burned with the fires of bitter resentment against this man whose blundering had wrought calamity.

CHAPTER XV

Even as the three outraged women moved forward slowly toward the door with that slowness which their dignity demanded of them under the circumstances, there came an interruption.

A servant appeared in the doorway, and then stood aside to usher in three newcomers. These were no others than Mr. McMahon, Mr. Schmidt and Mr. Ferguson, who halted in astonishment on the threshold, at beholding their wives thus unexpectedly bearing down on them in the house of the enemy. In their turn, the women came to an abrupt standstill, regarding the men with round eyes. For a few seconds, the six remained thus facing one another, too dumfounded by the encounter for speech.

Then, presently, the German uttered a guttural ejaculation in his own tongue, which seemed to relieve the general paralysis.

"Caught with the goods!" Ferguson exclaimed sardonically, with a scowl of rebuke directed toward his daughter.

At the same moment, McMahon fairly shouted an indignant question at his wife as to her presence in this house. But that Amazonian female did not shrivel before the blistering growl of her husband.

"Sure, I'll trouble you, Mike McMahon," she declared fiercely, "if it's endearing terms you're about to use, to wait till we get home." Under the spell of this admonition, the Irishman contented himself with subterranean mutterings, to which his wife discreetly paid no attention.

"But what's it all about?" Ferguson inquired sharply, of his daughter.

"Ah, forget it!" came the unfilial retort. Then, recalling the Vere De Vere, she amended her statement: "I mean, father dear, do not make a scene, I beg of you."

"A scene!" Ferguson exclaimed, savagely. "Why, I'll—"

What the irate Yankee might have done was never revealed, for he was interrupted by Cicily, who had now recovered her poise, so that she spoke pleasantly, favoring the tumultuous parent with her sweetest smile.

"Sadie and the other ladies came to call on me, Mr. Ferguson," she exclaimed, well aware that this announcement left the mystery of the women's presence as it had been before.

Mrs. McMahon, however, shed a ray of light on the puzzle.

"Faith, and 'tis that," she agreed, glibly. "We just dropped in for a cup of tea with a member of our club."

It was Hamilton who now interrupted further questions by the three husbands. He had been nervously fidgeting where he stood, and at last his impatience found vent in words.

"I'm not interested in these domestic affairs," he snapped. "If you men have anything to say to your wives and daughters, take them home, and say it to them there. This is not the place for it. There's only one thing that I have time to listen to from you."

Schmidt waddled forward a pace beyond his fellows, and addressed his former employer with the dignity born of constituted authority.

"Well, Mr. Hamilton," he said ponderously, with his accent more pronounced than usual by reason of the emotion under which he labored, "I speak as the chairman of the committee. So, sir, you will listen to us right here and now." He paused for a moment to wipe the perspiration from his forehead with an adequately huge handkerchief.

Ferguson seized on the opportunity thus given to voice the rancor that was in his heart.

"Yes, yes," he cried excitedly, "you want to understand that we're men! We're striking—yes! But we're fighting you in the open, like men. And we've come to tell you that we're not going to stand for the way you fight.... Is that plain enough for you, Mr. Hamilton?"

The amazement of Hamilton over the charge thus brought against him was undoubtedly genuine. He stepped forward as if to strike, but checked himself almost instantly. There was no longer any look of boyishness in the drawn fare, with the chin thrust forward belligerently, the brows drawn low, the eyes blazing.

"The way I fight!" he repeated challengingly, menacingly.

Schmidt, having restored the handkerchief to its pocket, took up the accusation.

"Yes," he declared, with surly spitefulness. "I have been in a dozen strikes, and this is the first time any employer ever attacked me in my affections— through my Frieda." The German's narrow eyes were alight with venomous resentment, as he glowered at Hamilton.

Astounded by this attack, Hamilton forgot rage in stark bewilderment.

"What on earth do you—can you—mean?" he stormed.

"It is not right," was the stolid asseveration of the German. "The home is sacred." The speaker's tone was so malevolent that Hamilton was impressed, in spite of himself. And then, suddenly, a suspicion upreared itself in his brain—a suspicion so monstrous, so absurd, so baseless, so extravagantly impossible, that he would have laughed aloud, but for the sincerity of the feeling manifested in the faces of the men before him. His eyes roved from Schmidt to the faded woman who was the man's wife. He saw her shrinking behind the ample bulk of Mrs. McMahon, her mouth opening and closing soundlessly, as if in a wordless soliloquy. Then, again, his eyes returned to the man who had just uttered the preposterous accusation, and he beheld the usually jocund face distorted by a spasm of jealous fury, the insensate fury of the male in the loathed presence of a rival. No, here was no room for laughter. However ludicrous the mistake in its essence, its fruits were too serious for mirth. He turned his gaze on McMahon, and saw there the like virile detestation of himself. He ventured a glance toward the Amazon, who loomed over-buxom and stalwart. Again, he was tempted to amusement; but, again, a look toward the husband checked any inclination toward lightness of mood. Finally, he regarded Ferguson, and there, too, he beheld a passionate reproach. He did not trouble to stare at the girl. He remembered perfectly her cheap prettiness, her mincing manner, her flamboyant smartness of apparel from Grand Street emporiums of fashion. The strain of a false situation gripped him evilly, so that for the moment he faltered before it, uncertain as to his course. Denial, he felt, must be almost hopeless, since how could men capable of such crude stupidity digest reason? He hesitated visibly, and in that hesitation his accusers read guilt.

It was evident from a sudden, flaming red that suffused Mrs. McMahon's expansive countenance that she was beginning to grasp the purport of the accusations against Hamilton. She started toward her husband with a demeanor that augured ill for peaceful conference, when she was stayed by Cicily's grasp on her arm.

"Wait!" came the command, in a soothing voice. "Let me speak to these foolish men. You'll only stir them up, and make them worse." The Amazon yielded reluctantly, for she loved as well as honored the woman who had won her friendship by so much endeavor; but there was dire warning of things to come in the gaze she fixed on her suspicious husband.

"I'll not listen to this foolishness any longer," Cicily declared, dearly, in a cold voice that held the attention of all. "You men are too utterly absurd. There's no love lost between your wives and my husband, I assure you. If you had chanced in a few minutes earlier, you would have been well aware of the fact." Her statement was corroborated by the vehement nods of the women and the glances of disdainful aversion that they cast on the master of the house at this reference as to the status of their mutual affection. "Your wives and daughters," Cicily concluded haughtily, with a level look at the three husbands, which was not wanting in its effect, "are my friends."

But Ferguson was not dismayed by the reproof.

"Yes, Mrs. Hamilton," he answered, with bitter emphasis, "you're the one— we know that! You're the cat's-paw, with your clubs and your benefits." He turned to Hamilton, and went on speaking with even greater virulence. "It's through her that you're fighting; it's through her that you're attacking us in our homes; it's through her that you're turning our wives and our daughters against us until our lives are miserable with them, morning, noon and night. They're forever talking against the strike, trying to make us come back to you, and to take the cut. And it ain't fair, I tell you! No honest employer would fight that way from behind a woman's petticoats. Women haven't got any place in business, according to our way of thinking. We didn't mind your wife's butting in with bath-tubs and gymnasiums and libraries, and such foolish truck as that; but, when it comes to mixing up in the strike, and organizing our wives and daughters against us, why, we kick. That's the long and the short of it, Mr. Hamilton. No real man would stoop to that sort of work. It's a woman's trick, that's what it is—and women have no place in business." Schmidt and McMahon, almost in unison, rumbled assent.

At last, the badgered employer felt himself sure of his ground.

"You're right, Ferguson," he declared, with intense conviction. "Women have no place in business. You don't need to argue to convince me of that fact. If you doubt my sentiments in that respect, just ask my wife—she knows what my ideas on the subject are. But I knew nothing of all this. Mrs. Hamilton has mixed herself up with this affair entirely without my knowledge or consent. She has nothing whatever to do with my business affairs. As for the future, you may rest assured—"

"You may rest assured," Cicily interpolated, "that Mrs. Hamilton will continue to do precisely as she pleases."

"But, Cicily—" Hamilton would have protested.

"Precisely as she pleases," came the repetition, with an added emphasis, which, Hamilton knew from experience, it would be useless to combat.

"Faith," exclaimed McMahon, in humorous appreciation of the scene, "the filly has the bit in her teeth and is running away."

Cicily, however, was not to be diverted from a frank exposition of her position. Now, she faced the men, and made clear her attitude:

"Let me tell you that Mrs. Hamilton is proud to be merely a member of the club which you have heard referred to and certainly she is not going to resign her membership in it. You men have your union. There's no reason why we women should not have our club as well. You say that I've been helping them. Very well, what of it? Yes, I have been helping them. Why shouldn't the women take money from me, I'd like to know. For that matter, it's nothing like what you men have been doing—taking money from Carrington and Morton.... And you talk about fighting fair!"

At the final statement made by his wife, Hamilton whirled on the men.

"What's that?" he fairly barked. "Are Morton and Carrington supplying you fellows with money to prolong the strike?"

"Yes," Cicily replied, as the men maintained a sullen silence. "And these men of yours have been listening to their lying promises about starting a new factory, as soon as you are down and out for keeps." She eyed the men scornfully, as she continued: "Haven't you the sense to see that it's merely a plan to ruin Mr. Hamilton completely? They want to kill him off for good and all. Then, when he's out of the way, you'll have to work for any sort of wages they are willing to give you. Good gracious, the scheme is plain enough! Why can't you see it as it is—a plot to do him up through you? A woman can see the inside of it easily enough!"

But her sensible argument was wasted on the men, who already had their opinions formed, and were not likely to change them readily at a word.

"Women have no place in business," Schmidt reiterated, heavily. "We have proved that. Now, Mr. Hamilton, you just keep your wife to yourself. We don't want her meddling around in our concerns. And we'll keep our wives to ourselves. They don't want you!" he added significantly; and McMahon and Ferguson endorsed the sentiment by vigorous nods of assent. "So," the German concluded, "we will settle this strike ourselves, like men, without any more woman's interference. Am I right?"

"That's exactly what I want you to do," Hamilton replied. "And any time you want to come back with the cut, let me know."

"I hope you won't hold your breath while you're waiting," the Irishman advised grimly.

"And I hope you won't be hungry," Hamilton retorted.

With this exchange of civilities, the meeting between the men and their former employer came to an abrupt end. Without any further farewells than a series of curt nods, the men filed from the room.

"I'm thinking that it's a pleasant talk we'll be having together, this night," Mrs. McMahon remarked judicially, after the departure of the committee.

"So, it's thinking I am that we'd better start early, and then we'll have time a plenty to thrash it out with the boys. Good-by, Mrs. Hamilton.... And please to remember that the next meeting of the club is to be on the Thursday."

"I'll surely be there," Cicily promised.

The adieux were quickly spoken, and the women took their departure, leaving husband and wife alone together, standing silently.

CHAPTER XVI

Hamilton stirred presently, turned, and threw himself heavily into the nearest chair, whence he stared curiously at his wife with morose eyes of resentment. Cicily felt the scrutiny, but she did not lift her gaze to his. She was not shirking the conflict between them, which seemed inevitable after this last episode; but she was minded to let her husband begin the attack. In her turn, she sought a chair, into which she sank gracefully, and rested in a pose of languid indifference that was fascinating in itself, but at this moment for some inexplicable reason peculiarly aggravating to the man. It may be that her apparent ease at a critical period in their fortunes appealed to him as hatefully incongruous; it may be that the gracious femininity of her, her desirability as a woman, thus revealed by the lissome lassitude of her body, emphasized the fact that she was a creature created for joy and dalliance, not for the rasping stratagems of the market-place. Whatever the cause, it is certain that the lazy abandon of her posture irritated him, and it was with an attempt to veil his chagrin that at last he spoke:

"Well," he exclaimed petulantly, "some more of your work, I see!"

Cicily, however, disguised the fact that she winced under the contempt in his tone.

"Yes," she answered eagerly. "Now, don't you see that I was right?"

The device did not suffice to divert Hamilton from his purpose of rebuke.

"So," he went on, speaking roughly, "not content with forgetting your duty, not satisfied with your dreary failure as a wife, you've turned traitor, too."

"You seem to forget that it was yourself who failed in your duty—not I," Cicily retorted.

"Is that trumped up, farcical idea, your excuse for fighting me?"

"I'm not making any excuses," Cicily replied, stiffly. "And for the simple and very sufficient reason that I am not fighting you."

"Then, what under heaven do you call it?" Hamilton demanded, with a sneer. "Is it by any chance saving me?"

"Yes, I'd do that," came the courageous statement, "if only you'd let me."

"And your manner of doing it," Hamilton went on, still in a tone of sneering contempt, "I suppose would be by going on the way you have been going— giving money to my enemies, and so prolonging the strike, and so ruining me!"

"I do believe you are blind!" Cicily declared, angrily. She changed her pose to one of erect alertness, and her eyes flashed fire at her husband. "Is it possible that you don't appreciate why I gave those women money—why I helped them? Why, I wouldn't be a woman, if I didn't. As I've told you before, I was a woman before I became a wife. If keeping other women and little children from going hungry isn't wifely, isn't businesslike, then thank God I'm not wifely, not businesslike!"

"Well, you're not, all right," Hamilton announced succinctly. "I'm glad that you're satisfied with yourself—nobody else is."

"Oh, I know what you want," was the contemptuous answer. "You want the conventional, old-time wife, the sort that is always standing ready and waiting to swear that her husband is right, even when her instinct, her brain, her heart, all cry out to her that he is wrong. Well, Charles, I am not that sort of wife, nor ever will be. The real root of the trouble is that we women are changing, developing, while you men are not: you are the same. We, as a sex, are growing up, at last; your sex is standing still. The ideas our grandmothers held, the lives they led, would kill us of dry rot. But you men are just where your grandfathers were in relation to your homes and your beliefs as to the duty of your wives. Of course, your old-time wife looked up to her over-lord with reverence; she hung on his every word with profound respect; she swore by his every careless opinion, without ever daring to call her soul or her mind her own. For that matter, why shouldn't she have done so? He was educated, after some sort of fashion at least; and he went abroad into the world, where he mixed with his fellows, where he did things, good or bad; while she, poor, pretty, ignorant doll, snatched up by him in early girlhood, and afterward kept sequestered, forced to assume the tragic responsibilities of a wife and mother before she was old enough to appreciate her difficult position—what chance did she have? Now, to-day, I tell you, it is all different. We're as well educated as you men—better, oftentimes. We have discovered that we can think intelligently; we do think. We, too, go abroad into the world; we, too, do things. Best of all, we see with a new, clearer vision. And we see certain things that you men have become blinded to through centuries of usage, of selfish, careless struggling for your own ends. We are able to see with the distinctness of truth the right relation of the man and the woman—an equal relation, with equal rights for each, with equal claims on each other, with equal duties to each other in the home and in the world outside the home—partners, held together by love."

"My dear," Hamilton remarked dryly, as his wife paused, "you have omitted one salient qualification of the modern woman: she is, preëminently an orator. Why, you, yourself, are a feminine Demosthenes—nothing less." But he abandoned, his tone of raillery, as he continued: "And so, what you've been doing—that's your idea of partnership, is it?"

"Yes," Cicily declared, spiritedly. "When one partner makes a mistake, it's the duty of the other to set things straight."

"By ruining him!" the husband ejaculated, in savage distrust.

"Have I ruined you?" There was a flame of indignation in the amber eyes, and the curving lips were turned scornfully; but there was a restrained timbre of triumph in the music of her voice. "No! Why, let me tell you something: Those women are for you, already. They are helping me against their husbands. You'll win in the end—in spite of all the damage you tried to do to-day with your colossal blundering. But they're loyal to me, and they'll forgive you for my sake, and they'll give you the victory in the fight.... Just wait and see!"

"Nonsense!" Hamilton mocked. He considered his wife's assertions as merely the maunderings of an extravagant enthusiast. She was sincere—more the pity!—but she knew absolutely nothing of the problems with which she insisted on entangling herself so futilely.

"I promise you," Cicily persisted, undismayed by her husband's jeering attitude of scepticism, "that you will win in the end. Yes, you will; because it is right: that you should. I am doing my part, not only to help you; but, too, because it is right. We owe a duty not only to ourselves, but to those people as well.... Even you must see that!"

"Well, I don't," Hamilton maintained, consistently. But he winced involuntarily under the expression of pity for his ignorance that now showed in his wife's face.

"Well, it only serves to illustrate what I said," Cicily went on, with a complacency that annoyed the man almost beyond endurance. "The woman has the clearer visions nowadays. That's where we differ from our dear departed grandmothers, from our mothers even. They had a personal conscience that stopped short at the front and back doors of the home. We women of to-day have a bigger conscience, which takes in the bigger family. It's a social conscience, and that it is which makes us different from those women of the earlier generations. Don't you see, Charles, that you and I are really a sort of big brother and sister to those in our employ? So, let us help them, even if we have to do it against their own mistaken efforts of resistance."

"Of course," Hamilton suggested, still sneeringly, "Morton and Carrington, too, are our dear brothers."

For an instant, Cicily was nonplused by the question; but, of a sudden, she received one of those inspirations on which she usually relied for escape from a predicament.

"Oh, yes, indeed," she replied happily, and beamed radiantly on her astonished husband, in anticipatory enjoyment of her repartee. "They're our bad brothers, whom we must spank—hard!"

"If there's any spanking to be done, I'll attend to it, myself," Hamilton declared, gruffly.

"Oh, very well," Cicily agreed. "But you don't seem to be doing it effectively at present.... Tell me, why are they paying the men to stay on strike?"

"It must be that they recognize the brotherhood claim of which you were speaking so eloquently." The man's voice was vibrant with sarcastic indignation.

"Now, see here, Charles," Cicily remonstrated, the flush in her cheeks deepening under the rebuff in his flippant answer. "You know why they're doing it just as well as I do. It's simply because they want to keep you closed down, so that they can go on charging the independents twenty-two cents a box."

"No," the husband declared, enticed despite his will into discussing business for a moment with his wife, "they could charge them that anyhow. I couldn't interfere, because they have me tied up with a contract at eleven cents."

"Then, if I were you," Cicily argued with new animation, "I'd break that contract. Yes, I'd open up right away, pay full wages, and sell to the independents at fifteen cents a box. They'd come to you fast enough."

"Break a contract with a trust!" Hamilton jeered. He laughed aloud over the folly of this idea as a means of escape from disaster.

"What are contracts when the men are starving?" The question came with an earnestness that did more credit to the heart than to the head of the wife.

"If that isn't like a woman!" The man's tone was surcharged with disgust. "Cicily, I've had enough of this."

"Then, you won't fight?" An energetic shake of the head was the answer. "You won't help the men?" Again, the gesture of refusal. "You won't make any move at all?" A third time, the man silently denied her plea. "Then, I will!" Cicily concluded, defiantly. She leaned back in her chair, clasped her slender hands behind her head, and stared ceilingward, with the air of one who has pleasantly solved all the perplexities of life.

"Good heavens, what do you mean to do next?" Hamilton questioned, in frank alarm.

"Never mind: you'll see," came the nonchalant answer.

The contented air of the woman, coupled with her tone of assurance as she spoke, goaded the man to an assertion of authority.

"I demand that, as long as you're in my house—"

He was interrupted by the cold voice of his wife. She did not turn her eyes from their dreamy contemplation of the ceiling, nor did she alter in any way the languor of her posture, the indifference of her manner. But, somehow, the quality in her voice was insistent, and the gentle, musical tone broke on his delivery with a subtle force sufficient to halt it against his will.

"You can't demand," Cicily said, evenly. "We stopped that relationship three weeks ago."

"It is true," Hamilton answered, more quietly, "that you've refused to live with me as my wife. But, if you are to remain in my house, I must insist that you keep out of meddling with my business affairs. Otherwise, I shall be forced—"

Again, the softly spoken words from his wife's lips held a spell that checked his own, and compelled him to listen grudgingly.

"You cannot force me, Charles—for the simple reason that I won't leave. No, indeed! I am quite certain that when you think things over in a saner mood, you will be convinced of the fact that just at this time it would be highly inadvisable for you to complicate your affairs further by a public scandal. So, I tell you that I sha'n't go. I shall stay here until you are out of this mess. Since I feel that to be my duty, I shall do it!"

"Oh, Lord, if you were a man—!" Hamilton choked helplessly.

"If I were a man," was the placid conclusion offered by Cicily, "I suppose I'd sit still, and do nothing, like you. But I'm not a man, thank Heaven!... The only pity is, you won't take my perfectly good advice."

"Your advice—oh, the devil!" Hamilton sprang from his chair. His face was distraught, as he stood for a moment staring in baffled anger at his wife, who still held her eyes meditatively content on the ceiling. He clenched his hands fiercely, and shook them in impotent fury. "Your advice!" he repeated, in a voice that was nigh moaning. Then, he whirled about, and strode from the room, trampling heavily.

Cicily listened until she heard the door of the library slam noisily. In the interval, she retained her attitude of consummate ease. But, with the sound of the closing door, she was suddenly metamorphosed. Her eyes drooped wearily. She cowered within the chair as one stricken with a vertigo. The slender hands unclasped from behind her head, and shut themselves over her face. Her form was bowed together, and shaken violently. There came the sound of muffled sobs.

CHAPTER XVII

In the days that followed, Cicily found herself on the very verge of despair. She had pinned the hope of success for her husband on a restored influence with the wives of the leaders in the strike. She had felt confident that, with them fighting in her behalf, she would achieve victory. She had not doubted that these women could mold the men to their will. Now, however, she had, to a great extent, lost faith in the efficacy of this method. She had seen and heard those husbands defy their womankind openly. They, too, were obstinate in their belief that women should not obtrude into business affairs. She realized that she was combating one of the most tangible and potent factors in human affairs, the pride of the male in his dominion over the female—an hereditary endowment, a thing of natural instinct, the last and most resistant to yield before the presentations of reason. The resolute fashion in which her husband held to his prerogative of sole control was merely typical. These other men of a humbler class were like unto him. Evidently, then, she must contrive some other strategy, if she would save her husband from the pit he had digged for himself by yielding to the specious processes of Morton and Carrington. Yet, she could imagine no scheme that offered any promise of success.... She grew thinner, so that her loveliness took on an ethereal quality. Her nights were well nigh sleepless; her days became long hours of harrowing anxiety.

She was sitting in her boudoir late one afternoon, still revolving the round of failure in her plans. She had dressed to go out; but, at the last moment, a wave of discouragement had swept over her, and she had sunk down on a couch, moodily feeling that any exertion whatsoever were a thing altogether useless. She was disturbed from her morbid reflections by the entrance of a servant, who announced the presence of Mr. Morton and Mr. Carrington in the drawing-room, who had called to see Mr. Hamilton. In sheer desperation, with no precise idea as to her course, Cicily resolved to interview these callers, since her husband had not yet returned home. So, she bade the servant inform the gentlemen that Mr. Hamilton was expected to return very soon, and that in the meantime she would be glad to give them a cup of tea. As soon as the servant had left the room, she regarded herself minutely in the mirror, made some adjustments to the masses of her golden brown hair, pinched her pale cheeks until roses grew in them, observed that her skirt hung properly, and then descended to the drawing-room, which she entered with an air of smiling hospitality, of luminous loveliness, of radiant youthfulness, calculated to beguile the sternest of men from their habitual discretion.

The two gentlemen rose to greet her with every indication of pleasure. As a matter of fact, they enjoyed the charm that radiated from the beautiful young woman, but, in addition, they rejoiced in this opportunity to gather from her carelessness some information that the reserve of her husband would certainly have withheld. It was with deliberate suggestion that Morton addressed her heartily as "Mrs. Partner," having in mind a former interview, in which she had so declared herself. But it was Carrington who, after the three were seated, and while waiting for the tea-equipage, ventured to introduce the topic of his desires directly by asking how business was.

"Oh, business is booming!" Cicily answered, with such a manner of enthusiasm that it hoodwinked her hearers completely. They uttered ejaculations of surprise involuntarily, but managed to refrain from any more open expressions of wonder. "Oh, yes, indeed!" Cicily continued, following blindly an instinct of prevarication that had been suddenly born within her brain. "Isn't it splendid? We just ended our strike to-day." She stared intently at Carrington with sparkling eyes. It filled her with secret delight to witness the expression of consternation on that gentleman's face; and she could not resist the temptation to add maliciously, although she veiled her voice: "I know that you're glad for us, Mr. Carrington. I can just tell it by looking at you."

"Er—oh—yes, of course," Carrington stammered hastily, the while he attempted a wry smile. He pulled his handkerchief from a pocket, and wiped his forehead.

"Yes, indeed; we're both delighted," Morton added quickly, to cover the too evident confusion of his associate.

"Ah," Cicily went on gloatingly, turning the iron in the wound relentlessly, "it does surely make you feel good when you win a strike, doesn't it? Next to an Easter hat, I think the winning of a strike is the grandest sensation!"

"So, you really won?" Morton inquired, half-suspiciously.

"Oh, yes!" Cicily assured him, with an inflection of absolute sincerity. Then, abruptly, the expression of her face changed to one of alarm, mingled with cajolery. "But, please, Mr. Morton," she pleaded, "you won't say anything about it, will you? Charles doesn't wish to have it announced just yet, for some reason or another."

"No, certainly not, Mrs. Hamilton," Morton assured her. "We won't tell of it."

"Thank you so much!" was the grateful response; and Cicily fairly dazzled the puzzled gentlemen by the brilliancy of her smile. "You know," she continued mournfully, "Charles did scold me so after you were here that other time when I talked to you. He scolded me really frightfully for talking so much.... It didn't do a bit of good my telling him that I didn't say a thing. But I didn't, did I?" She asked the question with the ingenuous air of an innocent child, which imposed on the two men completely.

"Indeed, you didn't!" Morton declared with much heartiness, as he darted a monitory glance toward Carrington. "Why, for a business woman, I thought you a very model of discretion, Mrs. Hamilton. And so did Carrington—eh, Carrington?"

"Exactly!" Carrington agreed under this urging of his master. "If all women in business were like Mrs. Hamilton here, business would not be so difficult."

Cicily felt the sneer in the words, but she deemed it the part of prudence to conceal any resentment. On the contrary, she assumed a hypocritical air of triumph.

"Good! I'll tell that to Charles," she declared, joyously. "You know he's such a horribly suspicious person that he doesn't trust anyone." Once again, she turned to Morton with an alluring smile. "Of course, he ought to be very glad, indeed, to trust you, his father's oldest friend."

"I hope that you told him that," Morton replied primly, albeit he was hard put to it to prevent himself from chuckling aloud over the naïveté of this indiscreet young woman.

Cicily maintained her mask of guilelessness.

"Yes, indeed, I did!... He said that was why he didn't trust you."

Morton saw fit to change the rather delicate subject.

"It must be a matter of great satisfaction that you have at last won this strike," he remarked, somewhat inanely.

"Of course, it is," Cicily agreed, with a renewal of her former enthusiasm. "Oh, I'm so glad, because now we can pay our men their old wages! That's how we won the strike, you know," she went on, with a manner of simplicity that was admirably feigned; "just by giving in to them. All we had to do was to give them what they wanted, and everything was all settled right away."

"Ahem!" Morton cleared his throat to disguise the laugh that would come. "Yes. I've known a good many strikes that were won in that same way."

Carrington, who had been ruminating with a puzzled face, now voiced his difficulty.

"To save my life," he exclaimed to Morton, "I don't see how Hamilton can pay the old wages, and deliver boxes at eleven cents. I couldn't do it!"

"Why, you see, that's just it," Cicily declared blithely, still following her inspiration with blind faith. "We're not going to deliver boxes at eleven cents."

At this amazing statement, the two men first regarded their hostess in sheer astonishment, then stared at each other as if in search of a clue to the mystery in her words. The entrance of a maid with the tea-tray afforded a brief diversion, as Cicily rose and seated herself at the table, where she busied herself in preparing the three cups. When this was accomplished, and the guests had received each his portion, Carrington at once reverted to the announcement that had so bewildered him.

"You say, you're not going to deliver boxes for eleven cents?" he said, tentatively.

"No," Cicily replied earnestly, without the slightest hesitation; "we're going to sell to the independents at fifteen. We've gone in with them, now." She felt a grim secret delight as she observed the unmistakable confusion with which her news was received by the two men before her.

"You say you've gone in with the independents?" Carrington repeated, helplessly. His mouth hung open in indication of the turmoil in his wits as he waited for her reply.

"Yes, that's it!" Cicily reiterated, with an inflection of surpassing gladness over the event. "Oh, it does make me so happy, because now, you see, we can all be genuinely friendly together. We're not competitors any more."

But now, at last, Morton's temper overcame his caution. He turned to Carrington with a frown that made his satellite quake; but the fierceness of it was not for that miserable victim of his machinations: it was undoubtedly for Hamilton, who, according to the wife's revelations, dared pit himself against the trust by violating his contracts with it.

"We'll see Meyers about this," Morton declared, savagely. "So, he'd go in with the independents, would he? Well, let him try it on—that's all!"

Cicily stared from one to the other of the two men, with her golden eyes wide and frightened.

"Oh," she stammered nervously, "did I—have I said anything?... Oh, my goodness, Charles will be so angry!"

She maintained her attitude and expression of acute distress, while the two men rose, and, very rudely, without a word of excuse to their hostess, moved to the far end of the drawing-room, where they were out of earshot. But, on the instant when their backs were turned, the volatile young wife cast off her mock anxiety, and, in the very best of spirits, wrinkled her nose saucily at the disturbed twain.... And, as long as they conferred together, with no eyes for her, she sat alertly erect, smiling to herself, as one highly gratified by the course of events.

"Now, if only Charles doesn't spoil things again!" she murmured.

CHAPTER XVIII

Morton and Carrington were just finishing their low-toned, but very animated, conference at the end of the drawing-room, when their attention, together with that of Cicily, was attracted by a noise at the door. All three looked up, to see Hamilton striding into the room. Behind him came Delancy. At a gesture of warning from his wife, Hamilton faced about, and saw his two business foes.

"Well, well, I didn't know that you were here," he exclaimed, with a fair showing of cordiality, as he advanced, and shook hands with the visitors. Delancy contented himself with bowing to each in turn, then went to Cicily, and asked for a cup of tea. During the few moments spent in offering this hospitality, Cicily whispered rapidly to the old gentleman, who appeared mightily startled at her words.

"Mrs. Hamilton has been entertaining us again," Morton remarked, in an acid tone, to his host. "Really, she has been rather more interesting than she was before."

At this statement, Hamilton shifted uneasily. He turned an indignant stare on his wife, wondering dismally what new imbroglio had been precipitated by her lack of restraint.

"Oh, you needn't look at me in that fashion," Cicily objected, with a pout. "I didn't say anything this time, either. I only told them about our winning the strike, and—"

"What!" Hamilton brought out the word like a pistol-shot.

"Surely, you couldn't mind my telling them that," Cicily said, in a voice suspiciously demure. "And that's all I told them, except—"

"Except what?" Hamilton fairly shouted.

"Why, except about the contracts to do the work for the independents at fifteen cents—that's all."

"You—you told them that!" the astounded husband gasped. He whirled toward Morton. "Why, it isn't so, Mr. Morton—not a word of it! You must realize that it isn't—that it couldn't be so."

Morton, however, was not convinced by the earnestness of the young man's repudiation. Instead, he looked his host up and down with a sneering scrutiny that was infinitely galling.

"I see," he said harshly, "that you're just like your father before you. He could always manage to contrive some way by which to accomplish his ends, without being over-troubled with scruples. Only, he would never have confided his business secrets to a woman."

Hamilton turned reproachful eyes on his wife.

"Cicily," he cried entreatingly, "I want you to tell Mr. Morton—"

But that resourceful woman interrupted him. Her face showed a shocked amazement, as she spoke swiftly:

"Charles, do you mean that you want me to—?" She did not finish the sentence; but the inference was so plain that Morton did not hesitate to make use of it.

"Trying to make your wife lie for you won't do any good, Hamilton," he advised, disagreeably.

But, if Hamilton had been perplexed before, he was now suddenly dazed by the inexplicable conduct of Delancy, who advanced nimbly from the tea-table, caught Hamilton by the arm, and drew him apart a little. He spoke hurriedly, in a low voice, but intentionally pitched so that Morton could overhear.

"It's no good, my boy," he declared, warningly. "You see, the fact of the matter is, you're caught—caught with the goods on, as the police say. And, when you're caught with the goods, don't waste time in lying. It makes a bad business worse, that's all." Having uttered these extraordinary words of advice to his marveling nephew, the old gentleman turned jauntily on the seething Morton. "Well, what are you going to do about it?" he demanded, composedly.

Morton, frantic over the trickery that, as he believed, had been attempted against him, made no pretense of suavity in this emergency. In his vindictiveness, he spoke with a candor unusual to him in his business dealings.

"Do?" he rasped. "I'll show you mighty quick what I'll do! You seem to forget, Hamilton, that we have a contract with you. You are under agreement with us to put all your work out for us at eleven cents a box."

Hamilton would have entered a violent protest against any purpose of evading his obligations; but Delancy silenced the young man by an imperative gesture, and took it on himself to reply, bearing in mind the whispered directions of his niece. He addressed Morton in a condescending fashion that was unspeakably annoying to that important personage.

"I never heard of any such contract," he declared blandly, "and I have a bit of money invested in the plant, too.... Has he one, Charles?"

"He has a verbal one," Hamilton answered, more and more bewildered by the progress of affairs. "He wouldn't give a written one."

"Huh! A verbal agreement!" Delancy sniffed. "Well, Morton, may I ask how you are going to work to prove this verbal agreement?"

"We'll show that he did the work at that price," was the aggressive answer. "That will suffice."

"Very good," Delancy said, judicially. "Only, Morton, I venture to predict that you can't prove your verbal contract—not by any manner of means....

Who was with you at the time when that verbal agreement was made between you and Hamilton, as you allege?"

Carrington, who had been almost as greatly puzzled over the course of affairs as was Hamilton, now perceived something that was definitely within his own knowledge.

"Mr. Morton and I were together," he vouchsafed.

"And, so, you met the two Hamilton partners?" Delancy queried.

Both Morton and Carrington denied that the wife had been present at the interview.

"I have an idea," Delancy continued imperturbably, "that Mrs. Hamilton here would be quite willing to go on the stand and swear that she was present at the interview with her husband, to which you have referred. From something she has let drop to me, I have a very strong impression to this effect." There was a whimsicality in the old gentleman's tone that none save his niece marked.

"But I tell you," Carrington vociferated, "she wasn't there!"

"I hardly see what that has to do with it," Cicily interpolated languidly, from her place at the tea-table. "I remember it all quite perfectly." There was a smothered ejaculation from Morton, which sounded almost profane; Carrington's eyes were widely rounded as he stared at his hostess. "Yes," she went on, her musical voice gently casual in its modulations, "I remember it so well, because it was the day after—after—oh, well, after something or other! I shall remember what presently. And I wore—"

"Never mind all that," Delancy interrupted. "It doesn't matter what you wore, or whether you wore anything, or not."

"Uncle Jim," Cicily cried, horrified. On this occasion, the emotion in her voice was wholly genuine.

But Delancy was in a combative mood, and eager to get on with the fight toward which he had been guided involuntarily by the whispered instructions of his niece.

"Morton," he inquired briskly, "have you read those recent decisions of Bischoff's on unfair contracts?" Then, as the other shook his head in sullen negation, the old gentleman went on complacently: "Well, I have—every word! Incidentally, the last one was against myself, so, naturally, I took a rather keen interest. Especially, as the Court of Appeals has just sustained it.... It happens, therefore, that I know what I'm talking about."

"If it's fight you want, you'll get it—more than you want, I fancy," Morton growled. "We'll put the price down to nine cents, and break you."

"You might as well put your price down to eight cents, while you're about it," Delancy retorted, with a chuckle. "You see, your price won't really matter a particle to us, since we have a fair—notice, please, that I said fair—contract at fifteen cents for five years, with a privilege of renewal at the same terms. Oh, yes, put your price down to eight cents, by all means!"

Carrington's face turned purple, as he heard the fleering announcement of his rival's success, and Morton betrayed signs of a consuming anxiety.

"Have you such a contract?" he questioned, more mildly than he had spoken hitherto.

Delancy turned to face Hamilton, and put the question bluntly.

"Have we, Charles?" There was no reply forthcoming from the distracted young man, only a burst of sardonic laughter. It seemed to him clear that everyone had gone mad together. Quickly, then, the old gentleman directed the question to his niece. "Have we, Mrs. Partner?"

"You bet we have!" Cicily answered on the instant, inelegantly, but with convincing emphasis.

A faint ray of illumination stole into the mental blackness of Hamilton. Under its influence, he addressed Morton with a half-sneer:

"Do you think any man would have the nerve to try bluffing on a thing like that?" In his thoughts there was a forceful emphasis on the word "man," but he carefully avoided letting it appear in the spoken word.

There followed a lengthy and acrimonious debate among the men, to which Cicily listened with an air of half-amused, half-bored tolerance. She was, in fact, thrilling with delight over her inspiration, which had at last come after such long waiting. She felt an intuitive conviction that her ruse would win the battle for her husband's success. She need worry no more over the powerlessness of her women allies to bend the husbands to their will. Hereafter, she would retain the friendship of those worthy women, but without any ulterior object beyond their own welfare. It appealed to her as vastly more fitting that triumph should come from duping these men, who were her husband's enemies, who would have ruined him by their schemes, but for her intervention with a woman's wiles where man's vaunted sagacity had proved itself utterly at fault. The sincerity of her belief had sufficed in a minute to win the coöperation of Uncle Jim, that most determined opponent to woman's intrusion on business affairs. He had listened to her suggestion at the tea-table, at first with scornful displeasure over her venturing an opinion of any sort on business. Then, as he comprehended the purport of her scheme, his instinct for finesse had caused him to seize on it impetuously, to act upon it immediately.... Surely, Cicily thought, since Uncle Jim had been won over, there remained only the working out of details to insure a glorious victory—her victory for Charles!

She aroused herself from her abstraction with a start of alarm as she heard Morton crying out defiance.

"I tell you," he was saying heatedly, "those independent people have contracts with us. All this plotting of yours is just damned foolishness—I beg your pardon, Mrs. Hamilton." The enraged capitalist flushed with new annoyance, for he prided himself greatly on the elegance of his manners, and it horrified him that he should have so far forgotten himself as to swear in the presence of a lady. "But they've no place in business anyhow!" he thought to himself consolingly.

"Oh, don't mention it!" Cicily answered, with an air of unconcern. To herself, she was reflecting amusedly on how much greater than the offender knew was his discourtesy toward herself, since she it was who was the author of that "damned foolishness" to which he had so feelingly referred.

But Delancy had no time to fritter away on niceties of etiquette.

"Oh, no, Morton!" he scoffed. "Johnson of the independents told me that you never gave them contracts, except for each lot. You see, that's how we got in on the deal."

"Yes, that's how we got in," Cicily echoed, in a gentle murmur. There was an infinity of satisfaction in her voice.

"We'll make them break with you," Carrington shouted, roughly.

"Just try it!" taunted Hamilton, who, at last, found himself embarked on this mad adventure in chicanery.

"I have five millions in negotiable securities," Delancy added. "I'm willing to spend every penny of it in 'busting' you, if you try it."

Hamilton now took up the argument, with a spirit that delighted the listening wife. It was evident to her that he had grasped the significance of her deceit, and was enthusiastic in following it up to the best of his ability.

"So," he said to Morton, "you fancy that you can make the independents leave us! Well, you'll learn your mistake presently. Do you suppose for a minute that they'll pass us up, when we offer a fair contract for fifteen cents, to deal with you, after you've just put the price up to twenty-two? Nonsense!"

Morton raised an imperatively restraining hand as Carrington was about to splutter some threat. Of a sudden, the diplomatic man of affairs resumed his gracious, suave bearing; and his voice was agreeably modulated when he spoke:

"Gentlemen, it seems to me that we're arguing a great deal, needlessly. Now, you know, both of you, that I always liked old Charley Hamilton. Well, as a matter of fact, I'm delighted to discover that his son here has the same quality of business ability. So, my boy, why shouldn't you come in with us? There's ample future for brains with us.... Of course, I'm saying this on the supposition that everything is just as you have represented it." The cold caution of the man of business cropped out in the concluding sentence.

"Make a proposition," Hamilton directed, curtly.

"Well," Morton replied, speaking with thoughtful deliberation, "we might take over a controlling interest in your factory for, say, two hundred and fifty thousand."

"Such an offer as that is merely a joke," was Hamilton's contemptuous retort.

"What do you think it's worth?"

"Conservatively, a million."

"Oh, absurd!" Morton exclaimed, reprovingly; but his voice retained its pleasant quality. "Dear me! Youth is so hasty! Now, my boy, the truth is that you know your factory isn't worth anything like that sum."

"I suspect that you have forgotten five fat years of prospective profits." There came a groan from Carrington at this reference, and Morton's face lost for a moment its wheedling amiability. But the latter's discomfiture was of the briefest, if one might judge by appearance.

"Is a million your lowest figure?" he demanded. Then, as a nod of assent from the owner answered his question, he added: "And a sixty-days' option goes with your offer?"

Hamilton, however, had other conditions to impose.

"If you take over the control," he asked, "do I stay in charge as president and manager? I must stipulate for that."

"Oh, well," Morton agreed graciously, "the brain that could pull off this deal ought to be of some use to us.... All right, my boy."

At this final statement from the magnate, Cicily could not forbear a subdued ripple of laughter. "The brain that could pull off this deal"—oh, splendid! Who now would dare deny that she was a partner in very truth, a partner worth while!... Then, her inspiration again urged her on. She was beset with feverish impatience, as the four men dallied tediously over their adieux. When, at last, the visitors were safely out of the house, the young wife bore down like a whirlwind on Delancy. She could not waste even a word on Hamilton yet.

"Quick! Quick!" she commanded. The red in her cheeks was deeper than it had been for weary weeks; her eyes shot fires of eagerness; her delicate fingers clutched the old gentleman's arm in a grasp so earnest that he winced from the pain of it.

"Eh, what?" he demanded, confused by the violence of her onslaught.

"Oh, do hurry, Uncle Jim!" Cicily cried. "The telephone—Johnson!"

"Good heavens, yes!" Delancy exclaimed, instantly aroused to the exigencies of the situation, while Hamilton stared blankly at the two conspirators. "I should say so! I've got to get hold of Johnson."

"He's on the wire by this time, I'm sure," Cicily announced. "While you were getting rid of those men, I sent Watson to call him up."

"Bully, Cicily!" Hamilton shouted, in irrepressible enthusiasm. For the first time, he had spoken honest praise of his wife's business ability, and the soul of the woman was filled with a glorious triumph.

Delancy was already on his way toward the telephone in the hall. But he turned to speak his mind:

"Why on earth don't your Aunt Emma have ideas like that," he questioned, resentfully; "practical ideas?"

"Perhaps she has," Cicily replied, accusingly. "But you would never listen." There was no answer beyond an unintelligible grunt from the old gentleman.

"Hurry! Uncle Jim!" Hamilton urged, in his turn. "And do your best. If Johnson's with us, the deal will go through. He's never gone back on his word, and he controls the independents."

"Yes, boy," Delancy cried over his shoulder, as he vanished through the doorway, "if he's with us, we—your wife—wins!"

"Anyhow," Hamilton soliloquized, "win or lose, it's a great game!"

Then, he turned to regard his wife, with eyes in which amazement vied with admiration.

CHAPTER XIX

Cicily, under her husband's intent gaze, felt a glow of embarrassment. To conceal her emotion, she turned, and seated herself in a chair, where she relaxed into a posture as listlessly indifferent as she could contrive in this moment of pleasurable turmoil.

Now, indeed, she realized that the moment of her vindication in this man's estimation was at hand. It was her brain that had evolved the ruse by which his enemies would be worsted. Delancy and Hamilton might still retain doubts as to the issue of the affair, but she had none. Her instinct, which had so ably guided her to this point, now assured her that victory was assured. It must be, then, that the husband who had treated her claims and pretensions so fleeringly would henceforth recognize her worth. He had been helpless in the grasp of circumstance, and the flood of disaster had threatened to overwhelm him. She had plucked him forth from the whirlpool, had brought him safe to shore. She had most nobly justified herself in the rôle of Mrs. Partner.... This was her hour of supreme delight. The lines of fatigue had vanished from the lovely face as if by magic; her eyes were happy, shining in a clear contentment; her scarlet lips were molded into a smile of joy, and from them a dimple crept to make a tiny shadow in the pale oval of the cheek.

As for Hamilton, that young business man found himself in a maze of perplexity, as he stood for a long time in silence, studying the fair picture of femininity there offered to his gaze. In his breast, various emotions warred lustily. He was a-thrill with elation over the possibility of outwitting the foes who had used every wile and subterfuge of trickiness to ruin him. He was moved to a profound admiration for the intelligence that had originated and carried out a counter plot so instantly effective in his interests. But underlying these was a grievous hurt to his egotism. The pride of the male was wounded sore. Where he, the head of the house, the lord of the home, the man of affairs, had ignominiously failed, that frail creature, his wife, whom he had criticised and rebuked time and again, had snatched victory from defeat by clever and unscrupulous machinations worthy of a master of high finance. This feat was something incredible, yet it was true that it had been achieved. It was something absolutely contrary to all the conventions in which he had been reared. It was directly opposed to his personal beliefs, as he had expressed them times without number, to all and sundry—notably to his wife. Here was the sting to his vanity. He had been wrong. Of that, there could be no doubt. In other cases, in all probability, his contentions would have been justified; but there was small consolation in this fact, since in his own vital concerns he had been proven wrong. He winced as he reflected on the humility that would be becoming on his part.... Then, he was moved to a sudden rapture, and forgot his hurt pride, as he realized again the exceeding worth of the woman whom he loved. Under the urge of this feeling, he exclaimed with candid vehemence of admiration:

"You darling little liar!" The fondness in his voice made the epithet a word of sweetest praise.

Cicily stirred animatedly, casting off her assumed listlessness, in the bliss of this honest tribute from him who had so sternly flouted her aforetime. Her eyes of gold lighted radiantly as they were lifted to his.

"Oh, no—a big liar, I'm very much afraid." She leaned forward, and her voice was gloating as she continued: "Oh, Charles, isn't it just splendid! And it was all so gloriously simple! Why, it isn't on my conscience one tiny little bit. You see, they lied, and so, of course, I was justified in lying. It was to save you, and to help our workers down there. So, I lied, and I'm glad of it." She gurgled unrestrainedly for a moment. "Do you know, Charles, dear, a woman can beat a man lying, any time!... Oh, it's great!"

But Hamilton, not being under the thrall of intuitions, was not yet ready to rejoice over a victory that remained to be won.

"Wait," he admonished. "You know, we haven't heard from Johnson yet. We don't know what he'll do."

"Pooh!" Cicily retorted confidently, for in her wisdom she accepted the dictum of her instinct without reserve. "If it should be necessary, why, I'll convince him, too."

His curiosity prompted Hamilton to ask a leading question.

"How did you come to think of it?" he inquired eagerly.

"Oh, I just thought of it because—because—" Cicily halted, completely at a loss. She knew very well how she had come to think of it. The idea had been the kindly gift of intuition—that was all there was to it. But the explanation of the fact to a mere man, with his finical dependence on logic and all manner of foolishness in the way of reasoning, offered considerable difficulty. So, she rested silent, puzzling over a means for making the truth lucid to a member of the non-intuitional sex.

"Well, because what?" Hamilton repeated, suggestively.

"Why, just because—" Unable to find adequate words for interpreting the cause, Cicily attempted a diversion. "And, anyhow, I'm so glad! Now, you do see that I can help you, that I can do something for you that counts." For the life of her, the young wife could not resist a temptation to boast a little over her accomplishment in the world of business. She even ventured to hint as to the "because" which she had left unexplained. "Surely, Charles, now you must see how it's possible for us women to help our husbands outside the home—once in a while, at least. Really, there is some room in business on occasion for intuition, just as there is in other things. But the few men who possess the gift don't call it by its right name—not they! I imagine they're too busy and prosperous to call it anything."

"You mustn't think I'm not grateful, Cicily," Hamilton answered, with surprising meekness. "I know how much I shall owe you, if this deal goes through." He went to the chair where his wife was sitting, and kissed her tenderly. "Yes, you'll find me grateful enough," he repeated earnestly, as he straightened again, and stood regarding her with lover-like intentness.

Cicily, however, was not wholly content with the expression of feeling on her husband's part. Her ambition toward really sharing his whole life was not to be thwarted by accepting a single success, and the resultant gratitude on the part of the one served, as a sufficient achievement.

"It's not gratitude that I want, Charles," she declared, resolutely; "that is, not gratitude alone. I want recognition."

"But I do recognize everything, Cicily," Hamilton urged, manifestly at a loss to understand his wife's precise meaning. Then, of a sudden, his vision cleared, and he spoke with a new gentleness, yet with something of the old authority. "I recognize most clearly that here and now is the real turning point of our lives. We have both made mistakes—"

"Oh, both?" Cicily questioned, rebelliously. Her serene confidence in herself did not relish the open confession of error.

"Yes," Hamilton maintained, judicially; "we've both made mistakes. I've cared too much for business. I admit that fully and freely. I let it intrude on my home life; I let it hamper the expression of my love for you. As for you, you adorable creature, you've been headstrong beyond belief. You've been impulsive to the limit of that very impulsive temperament of yours. You've been unreasonable to the verge of distraction. But, thank heaven! you've been—as you'd call it—intuitional, too. That redeems you from criticism— as it may redeem me from ruin in my business. So, darling, isn't it fair, when I say that I'm going to change, to say that I want you to change, too? To sum it up, dear heart, we must begin all over again."

Nevertheless, Cicily, although she was a-quiver with delight over the open revelation of her husband's changed feeling toward her and toward himself, did not hesitate to combat his determination. She shook her head slowly in negation of his proposal, and spoke with the energy of profound conviction:

"It's too late, Charles. We can't go back."

"But, Cicily," Hamilton remonstrated, greatly hurt by her resistance to his humble resolve, "you don't understand! I admit that I was wrong—more than partly to blame, perhaps." That was as far as he could go. The wife who loved him smiled secretly at the obvious effort with which he acknowledged so much. It was enough to satisfy her in that direction—more than enough! But there remained still the fact that she was totally out of harmony with his scheme of turning backward to begin their life together afresh, after a finer plan of conduct.

"There's no such thing as going backward in life, Charles," she declared, intently. "We must go forward—only forward!"

"No," Hamilton answered, gravely. "That would never do. The old struggle would come up again. You were right in your argument, Cicily, and I see it now. I recognize the existence of that modern triangle, as you described it. One must choose, inevitably. It's either you or business. I chose once, and I went wrong. Now, let me choose again, dear. Oh, you must believe me, sweetheart. You are the dearer—infinitely the dearer to me! It is you I love— only you!" There was genuine passion in the man's voice. It rang heavenly harmonies in the soul of the wife. For the moment, she was half-inclined to throw away the troubles begotten of ambition, the strivings engendered by ideals, to rest content with the happiness of love's transports. She fought the temptation stoutly, but it was almost beyond her woman's strength to resist. She feinted for time by haphazard questioning, voiced in broken, uncertain tones while she strove to maintain her purpose:

"What are you going to do, Charles? How will you prove that I am dearer to you, after all, than is this hateful business?"

"How am I going to prove it?" Hamilton repeated, with immense self-satisfaction. "Why, I'm going to sell out to Morton, to-morrow."

At this explicit statement of his purpose, Cicily was swiftly recalled from her temporary mood of yielding.

"You're going to quit?" she demanded, sharply. "Is that what you mean, Charles?"

"Yes," came the complacent answer, firm in the intensity of sudden resolve. "I have it all planned out, already. We'll take a steamer the last of the week for another—a better, wiser—honeymoon. We'll go to the Italian lakes, to Switzerland. Then, afterward, we'll drop down to that little village in the south of France. You remember the place, don't you, dearest?"

"Yes," Cicily answered, very softly. Her cheeks were flushed with tender memories of that embowered nook which had given lotos-eating pause to their wedding-journey. Her eyes were dreamy with fond reminiscence, as she imagined again the quaint beauties of that lover's paradise. But, by a fierce effort of will, she threw off the spell that threatened to defeat her most cherished ambition; and she spoke with an accent of supreme determination, in a voice become suddenly vibrant with new energy. "But I won't go!" Her face, too, had lost the delicate, yielding lines of the woman wooed and won, rejoicing in submission; it was again alert, set to fixedness of plan that would brook no denial. At sight of the change in her, Hamilton stared in dismay. He could not understand this development in her. He had humiliated himself in vain. He had offered the abandonment of all that could offend her, yet she remained obdurate, discontented, defiant of his every desire. He almost groaned, as he cast himself disconsolately into a chair, and buried his head in his hands, despairing of any understanding as to the whims of a woman.

"Don't you see, dear," Cicily went on, gently persuasive, "that we can't—we just can't!—quit? Why, Charles, being a quitter is the one thing that you've most hated all your life. And I, too, have hated it. No, you can't quit, because you're held here by duty—by duty to yourself, by duty to those men and women, our little brothers and sisters, who depend on you for their livelihood."

"The trust will take care of them," Hamilton declared mechanically, without lifting his face from his hands.

"You know how the trust will take care of them," Cicily retorted, with a touch of bitterness. "It will pay them a starvation wage—no more!"

"But you're jealous of business!" Hamilton objected, raising his head to gaze curiously at this most paradoxical person. "And, now, you are urging me to keep at it. I don't understand."

Cicily laughed aloud, in genuine enjoyment. Her eyes were alight with the fires of victory.

"I used to be jealous of it," she admitted, joyously. "I'm not any longer—because I've beaten it. Your offer just now proves that, doesn't it?... But, now that I have won a triumph over my old rival, why, we've got to go forward."

"Together?" There was a tender, half-fearful doubt in the husband's voice as he asked the question that meant so much to him, for he loved this variable wife of his in this moment more than he had ever dreamed that he could love a woman.

The wife's head drooped shyly, and her face flamed. Her word came very softly spoken, but it rang a peal of happiness in the heart of her husband.

"Yes."

The man rose from his chair, and went to his wife's side, where he stooped, and took her face in his hands, and raised it until he could look deep into the eyes of gold.

"You will care again, as you used to care?"

And she answered bravely, although a gentle confusion held her all a-tremble:

"I will care because—because I've never stopped caring!"

"Thank God!" Hamilton said reverently, and gathered her into his arms.

Afterward, the twain lovers talked of many things, as lovers will, of things grave and gay, of things silly and profound. They talked of business affairs, into which Cicily might on occasion flash the light of intuition to clear the way for grosser reason. They discussed the mutuality of interests that would be theirs, a lesson of supreme worth to a conventional world. They arranged philanthropic schemes for the betterment of conditions for the little brothers and sisters who gained a sustenance by toil at their behest. But, most of all, they talked those divine absurdities that are the privilege of all true lovers. The husband bewailed the incredible stupidity that had led him into neglect of the most adorable being in the universe; the wife mourned over the stern necessity that had driven her to sacrifice ineffable happiness on the altar of conscience.

They drew apart a little, when Delancy came bustling in from his conversation over the telephone; but they scarcely had ears for his jubilant announcement of victory.

"Johnson thinks it's great!" the old gentleman cried, triumphantly. "He's coming right up here in his machine, with a lawyer, to draw the papers.... And I've 'phoned for our attorney to get here as fast as he can. My boy, we've got 'em! Hooray!"

Hamilton responded with a perfunctory enthusiasm, but his eyes never left his wife's face.

As for Cicily, she sat silent, her eyes veiled, reveling in the glad riot of her thoughts. Through her brain went echoing the words spoken by her Aunt Emma, which had served in a measure to guide her course of action, and she smiled in perfect content as she mused on their meaning in her life. She had sought "to make other people happy." She had striven valiantly in behalf of the workers in the factory; she had struggled for her husband. Well, she had succeeded for them—surely, she had made other people happy; and out of her labors for those others she had won the supreme happiness for herself.

But it was after Delancy had left them that Hamilton reached into the inner pocket of his waistcoat, and plucked forth a little packet of tissue paper, which he unrolled with a touch that was half-caressing. Of a sudden, Cicily, watching, uttered a cry of delight.

"You cared—so much?" she questioned, with shy eagerness, as she put out her left hand.

The husband slipped the wedding-ring to its place.

"I cared so much," he said softly; "and infinitely more!"

The amber eyes of the wife were veiled with tears, as she lifted them to his.

"Oh, thank God, it is back again!" she whispered.

THE END

CPSIA information can be obtained
at www.ICGtesting.com
Printed in the USA
LVHW040600081222
734780LV00030B/1062

9 789356 716032